OUT WITCH THE OLD

A BLAIR WILKES MYSTERY

ELLE ADAMS

My dad and I waited to greet the company of fairies as they approached the town, moving down the grassy hill in a close-knit unit. There were three of them, a husband and wife with a daughter of around ten, all with the long hair and pointed ears that painted them as fairies. If that didn't give enough of a clue, they all flew on gossamer wings instead of walking, while glitter streamed in their wake.

At my feet sat Sky, my sort-of-familiar—he objected to the term 'pet,' but fairy cats were more independent than your regular witch's cat. He resembled a regular feline, but his eyes—one blue, one grey—gleamed with almost human intelligence. While he was indifferent to most humans, he'd insisted on tagging along to meet every new batch of fairies who'd shown up in town, and there'd been quite a few lately. I could credit that to Conor, my dad's old friend, who'd been gradually contacting all the other fairies he was acquainted with and seeing if they'd be interested in moving here to Fairy Falls.

The three newcomers wore wary expressions that relaxed a little when they saw I'd put on my own fairy appearance to greet them, complete with the glittering wings behind my back. They didn't know I was half human, half fairy, with a foot in both worlds, because in fairy mode, I resembled my dad almost exactly. He and I shared the same long dark hair, while his pointed ears contrasted with the human ones I usually wore as part of a glamour that had been put on me from childhood to enable me to blend in among the ordinary humans I'd grown up alongside. Now I was free to switch back and forth between fairy and human to my heart's content.

"Hey," I said to the newcomers as they halted in front of us. "I'm Blair Wilkes. Welcome to Fairy Falls."

"I am Braden Eventide," my dad said, and a murmur of recognition travelled among their group.

"My prince," murmured the man, bowing his head so his hair hung on either side of his face in long curtains. I hovered awkwardly in the background as they took in the sight of the once-fairy prince standing beside his half-human daughter.

Yeah. My dad was a fairy prince. It'd taken some getting used to, that was for sure.

"There's no need for that," said my dad. "I am a prince no longer. I live here now."

To my eternal surprise, prince or not, he'd elected to live in our sleepy town in the middle of nowhere and had already made the forest his home. Literally, because I suspected he'd used fairy glamour to create the new house that had appeared in the woods shortly after his arrival in town. More houses had soon popped up to join it as more fairies moved to town, since so far, most of the newcomers had opted to live in the same part of the woods.

My dad and I led the newcomers along the path that led to the section of the woods he'd picked out as his home—donated by the witches, at Madame Grey's request, to make up for their predecessors' decision to drive the fairies out of town hundreds of years ago. Conor had also had to get permission from the Elf King and Chief Donovan of the local werewolf pack to create a shortcut to the fairies' part of the woods in the form of a path that was invisible to the regular eye. If I hadn't had the ability to see through glamour, I'd have simply walked straight through the bright, twisting path without noticing it existed. As it was, my dad and I took the lead and stepped onto the winding road, which had once been part of Whitethorn Street, where Conor's house lay under a glamoured illusion he'd created so that nobody would be able to find him.

At the time, I'd been floored to realise any other fairies lived in the town at all, but I never would have imagined my dad and I would soon be leading the effort to help create a space for the descendants of the exiled fairies to return to their former home. Then again, until recently, I'd given up hope of ever seeing my dad in person at all. He'd been serving a lifelong sentence in jail for stealing the Seeing Stone from the regional witch council in order to hide it from the leader of the paranormal hunters. The hunters' leader, who happened to be a fairy himself, had wanted to use the stone to further his own ambitions, but I'd exposed him as a fairy and a fraud to his fellow hunters. While my dad had been freed from prison, the

Inquisitor had gone on the run and hadn't been seen by anyone since.

Regardless, a lot of fairies were understandably wary of moving to a town that had been fairy free for longer than most of the town's inhabitants could remember. For that reason, Conor had expanded the illusion around his house to create an entirely new section of the woods for the fairies in the same way that the werewolves, vampires, and witches had their own regions. As I'd learned the hard way when I'd brought my particular brand of chaos to town, most fairies felt like outsiders even among other paranormals.

The bright path, dappled with sunlight, soon led us to a clearing in which a number of neat cottages lay. All except one were occupied.

"We're going to need to expand this area at this rate," I commented. "Or else we'll run out of space."

"It's a glamour," said my dad. "It'll be fine. We can make as much space as necessary without needing to intrude on the witches' part of the forest."

"Ah." I still didn't quite get how the weird bubble universe worked, but it'd enabled the fairies to have somewhere to live where they weren't surrounded by a crowd of curious onlookers. It'd take a while for the novelty factor to wear off for some of the locals, but here, the peaceful sound of the falls filled the background along with the chatter of birds in the trees, while a soft breeze barely stirred the tranquil scene before us. Spring was in progress, and summer would follow fast on its heels, evident in the wildflowers growing at every corner and the clouds of insects in the air.

Conor strode out of one of the houses to greet the new

family, his long hair flowing in the breeze and his wings out.

"Welcome," he said to the newcomers. "You're moving to Number 16, right?"

"Correct," said the male fairy. "I'm Alden. This is Chrys, my wife, and Sparrow, our daughter."

"It's a pleasure to meet you. I am Conor Underwood."

He beckoned for them to follow him towards a neat cottage surrounded by wildflowers. Like its neighbours, the house gleamed lightly with a sheen of glamour, and Conor wasted no time in giving them a rundown of its features, all creations of his seemingly infinite talent for glamour. I had to admit it warmed my heart to see the fairy making friends with the newcomers. He'd been alone for years before I'd found him.

Then again, my dad had also been alone during his imprisonment. We'd been catching up on the missing years during the last couple of months, but he'd been out of touch with the rest of his relatives since long before he'd been jailed. I got the impression they hadn't approved of his union with my mother, a witch who also happened to be descended from the very coven who'd banished the fairies from the Falls and who hated exiles like my dad. He hadn't been back to the fairies' realm since.

'Complicated' was a mild way to describe my family history, but since most of my witch relatives were long gone, with the exception of Blythe and her mother, I felt zero kinship with the people who'd banished the fairies from town. Didn't make the other fairies less wary around the witches—even my dad, who admittedly had good reason to avoid the regional witch coven, since it'd been his theft of their Seeing Stone that had seen to his long imprisonment. I'd heard from more than one source that the Stone had once belonged to the fairies before the witches, but it wasn't as if anyone had proof. Besides, I was more concerned with keeping it out of the hands of Inquisitor Hare than anything else.

My dad smiled as the fairies entered their home behind Conor. "Let's leave them to it."

We continued past the large house my dad had chosen as his own until we came to the place where the path emerged into the main part of the forest. The sound of voices came from nearby, and when we emerged from the woods near a road lined with cosy cottages, a group of large, grey-skinned people blocked the way down the road. Gargoyles. Sky let out a low hiss, and his fur stood on end, while I came to an abrupt halt.

"Is that the police?" asked my dad.

"Yes." While they weren't currently in their winged and grey forms, the gargoyles were all tall and intimidating, especially since they comprised the town's entire police force. A slightly more welcome sight among them was my boyfriend, Nathan, an ex-hunter who now worked for the town's security force.

Nathan's expression tightened with worry when he spotted me, but he managed a smile. "Hey, Blair."

"What's going on?" I asked, walking over to him.

"There's been an incident," he said. "A girl has disappeared somewhere in the woods."

"A human girl?" asked my dad.

The gargoyles all eyed his wings in a way I didn't like. Not everyone was pleased about Fairy Falls's new inhabitants, and Steve and his fellow gargoyles already hadn't been my biggest fans.

"Yes," said the gargoyle I usually referred to as Ink Face. He'd earned the nickname when he'd barged into my place of work and been attacked by the office printer, and even now, the faint traces of inky blots remained on his craggy face. "A human girl called Laurel Hansen has disappeared in the fairies' part of the forest."

"Are you sure?" I asked. "The fairies' part of the forest is hard to get into if you can't see through glamour. It's not easy to wander into it by accident."

To be honest, it was a surprise that people didn't go missing in the forest more often, considering that its confusing paths seemed to look different every time I came in here… but the fairies' glamour wasn't to blame for that.

"Well, she's not here," Steve said. "We've searched thoroughly."

"Who was she with when she disappeared?" I asked. "Was she alone?"

"She was playing in her back garden the last time she was seen," Nathan said. "Her family's back garden is right in front of the woods."

My heart gave a stutter of unease. The woods weren't exactly a safe place for a child to play, mostly because of how easy it was to get lost and end up in trouble, but the fairies were the least of the dangers one might run into.

"Have you told the werewolves?"

"Not yet," said Nathan. "There's also the elves, whose territories are closer."

"They'd never harm a human child," said my dad. "I

have no doubt the elves would return her home if they stumbled upon her. The fairies would do the same."

Steve didn't look convinced, but I knew the elves were trustworthy. They'd helped my dad escape the hunters once, after all.

"Whatever the case, she's missing," said the gargoyle. "Which means we have to speak to everyone who was present in the area, including you."

"Me?" Should have seen that one coming. "We haven't seen any humans. We were just helping a new fairy family move to their new home."

"Then they ought to check they don't have a stowaway."

Typical. "I guess we can look around their part of the forest, but I'm pretty sure they'd have noticed a human wandering around."

Sky meowed at my feet, while Dad nodded. "Of course. I'm sure she hasn't gone far."

I retraced my steps down the forest path, worry beginning to rise inside me. A girl had disappeared near the fairies' new territory? This wasn't a good omen.

"You don't think she ran into trouble, do you?" I asked my dad.

"I don't know," he said. "Not in this part of the forest, I wouldn't have thought. Conor and I worked hard to make this place safe."

"Yeah." Safe for fairies didn't necessarily mean safe for humans, though. The aggressive flowers in Conor's garden came to mind, as did the goblin fruit my foster parents had once fallen victim to. Magic as a whole was unpredictable, and when you put multiple paranormals in the same place, it became even more so.

Yet I didn't believe for an instant that the fairies would have done anything to intentionally harm the humans who shared their forest, not when they'd waited years to be able to move back to their former home. I kept my fingers crossed that the missing girl would safely turn up as soon as possible.

2

An hour of searching the woods brought no results. My dad and I traversed every path around the area of the forest immediately behind the house where she'd last been seen until our steps brought us back to the fairies' part of the woods.

By now, most of them had come out of their houses, drawn by the background noise, and watched with wary eyes as Steve and the other gargoyles approached them. Steve had avoided this part of the woods up until now, but everyone knew him by reputation. It didn't help that the gargoyles couldn't fly in the forest, so they had to lumber around in an even more conspicuous manner than usual, trampling flowers and swearing at trees and generally being a nuisance.

Two young women who'd moved to the town a couple of weeks ago eyed the gargoyles from the doorways of their neighbouring cottages. Ani and Rosalyn were also the first fairies I'd met who were close to my own age, and

I'd been trying to find them new jobs via Dritch & Co since they'd moved in.

Ani waved at me when she saw me nearby. Her blond hair was almost white and cloud soft to match her wings. "Hey, Blair. What's going on?"

"A human girl disappeared in the forest." I approached her cottage, one eye on the lumbering gargoyles behind me. "Steve's got it into his head that she found her way here, but I have my doubts."

Rosalyn, dark haired and slender, wore an expression of irritation at the sight of Steve trying to disentangle himself from a creeping vine he'd walked into. "*That's* the chief of police?"

"I don't think there were many applicants for the position." I kept my voice low, while Sky the cat positioned himself defensively in front of the fairies' cottages. When Steve reached the clearing, I addressed him. "There are no human children here. I'm pretty sure someone would have noticed."

"You've got that right," Rosalyn returned from behind me.

Ani, not quite as bold as her friend, retained an air of wariness as the gargoyle cast a disapproving stare around the area. "We haven't seen any children except for the girl who just moved here."

"What girl?" said Steve.

"My dad and I helped a new family move here today," I said. "Their daughter's a fairy, but they haven't even met any of the other residents yet."

Not getting the message, Steve stalked around the clearing, glaring at everyone, while I tensed at the sound of a commotion from behind the gargoyles. A squat woman strode up to join them, breathless and red-faced. Her dark hair was tangled, and her glasses had steamed up from exertion.

"They took her!" she shrieked. "The fairies took her!"

Taking a wild guess that she was the mother of the missing girl, I walked in her direction, my ears protesting at her shrill yells. Nathan caught up with her, saying, "Please calm down, Mrs Hansen."

"The fairies didn't take anyone," I said.

Her gaze snapped to me. Too late, I remembered I still had my wings out and was otherwise indistinguishable from the other fairies. "Your people took my daughter. I know what you fairies do. You steal human children and leave your own in their place."

What in the world had given her that idea? "That's absurd. Nobody here is trying to steal anyone's kids."

She ignored me, addressing Nathan instead. "You know how dangerous those fairies are, don't you? They took her, mark my words."

"You have no proof whatsoever to back up that accusation." How he managed to be so patient with her was a mystery to me. "I will do what I can to find your daughter, but it's entirely possible that she wandered off into the woods and got lost. It's happened before."

"Not since *they* came here." She turned to Nathan with an ingratiating smile. "I'm sure you're doing your best. I know you felt pressured to make these freaks feel welcome, but…"

"Excuse me?" I interrupted.

She cut straight through me. "But decent people live here, too, and we've been in town for generations."

"The fairies lived here before the witches drove them

out." I couldn't seem to stop babbling, but the rest of the fairies could hear every word she said, and despite her obvious distress, we'd have noticed if her daughter was hiding among the cottages by now. "The newcomers just want to live in peace, nothing more."

She scoffed. "The hunters had the right idea if you ask me."

Her gaze went to Nathan again, and my heart pitched downward. She was being nice to him because she assumed that he held the same views as some of the hunters did. That definitely wasn't the case, but I'd hoped we'd seen the last of the hunters' habit of treating certain paranormals as inhuman, especially after their leader had been revealed as a fairy in disguise. I was tempted to remind her of Inquisitor Hare's big secret, but that probably wouldn't do anything to mitigate her anti-fairy crusade.

At that moment, a warning rumble of thunder in the air drew my attention to Conor, who stood nose to nose with Steve the gargoyle. "I did not steal any human children. How dare you accuse us of such crimes?"

Oh, no.

Leaving Nathan and Mrs Hansen, I trod towards Conor. The fairy's infamous temper had remained hidden over the last few weeks, but I hadn't quite forgotten the times he'd scared the crap out of me by unleashing a magical lightning storm, and I highly doubted a display of his magic would win him any favours with Steve or Mrs Hansen.

"You *did* steal the Seeing Stone," Steve said to Conor.

Ah. That was technically true, though it'd been my dad who'd given the stone to him for safekeeping, and there was a world of difference between a dangerous magical artefact and a human child.

"It was I who took the Seeing Stone." My dad stepped out onto the path behind the gargoyles. "Conor promised to watch it for me until it was safe to return the Stone to the witches. However, that is irrelevant to your current dilemma. I will allow you to search our territory for the missing child if you would kindly agree not to insult or threaten anyone."

The gargoyle glared at Conor. "You hid here for years without revealing your presence to anyone in town. How do I know you haven't been plotting against us?"

"Don't be ridiculous." I walked over to join my dad. "Conor lived in hiding because the hunters kept coming to town, and they wanted the fairies gone. Now they've stopped interfering in Fairy Falls, the fairies are able to live freely in a way they haven't for centuries. They wouldn't ruin their chances by capturing human children even if they had a reason to. Which they don't."

Steve growled under his breath, "This has nothing to do with you, Blair Wilkes."

"If you're going to accuse the people I just welcomed to town of committing a crime with no proof, it's my business," I pointed out. "The girl is probably lost somewhere in the woods. You should be searching for her, not interrogating people who've just moved here."

The gargoyle's face flushed an ugly red. "If an accusation is made, as Mrs Hansen did, it's my job to investigate her claims."

More like he wanted an excuse to stomp around the forest and intimidate the newcomers — and Conor, against whom he held an unending grudge for having had the audacity to stay hidden in the woods for years without anyone knowing he was there.

"Then by all means, search the territory," said my dad. "We'll wait here. Right, Conor?"

Conor's mouth parted, a hint of danger momentarily entering his expression. Then his face went blank. "If you insist."

I mouthed, *Please don't turn him into a tree,* but the fairy paid me zero attention. I didn't like his worrisome lack of reaction, but it was better than a spontaneous thunderstorm.

Apparently oblivious to the potential danger, the gargoyle stomped over to the nearest house, which happened to be Conor's. "I'm going to have to search this property."

Conor's irate reply turned into laughter when Steve bumped his head on the low doorframe on the way in. A series of thuds followed as he barrelled down the hallway, while his fellow gargoyles lumbered around the clearing. Fortunately, they opted to leave the other houses alone, but they insisted on searching the gardens.

To no one's surprise, the missing girl didn't reappear, though her mother continued to rail against the fairies to anyone who'd listen. That meant Nathan, who she followed like a shadow despite his refusal to give her his attention. I found myself glad I'd opted out of inviting him to meet the other fairies out of concern that they might take the presence of an ex-hunter as a sign that they weren't welcome in town. I'd wanted to build up to introducing them to one another, but now the gargoyles had effectively taken our progress back to zero.

Steve shoved his way out of Conor's house, nearly

knocking the door out of its frame in the process. "The child isn't in there."

"I told you," Conor said flatly. "You're wasting your time here."

"They hid her away!" Mrs Hansen shrieked, growing more and more visibly agitated with each passing minute. "The fairies have cast a spell on her."

"Come with us, Mrs Hansen," said Nathan with exaggerated patience. "Our team will keep searching the forest, and you're welcome to help us look."

"But she's here!" She dug her heels in and refused to move. "I know she is."

"Come on," Steve growled to her. "If we find any further evidence, then we'll return here to look for her."

"But..."

"Enough." Nathan stepped in. "Your daughter is most likely lost somewhere in the woods, and if we want to find her before nightfall, we'd greatly appreciate your help."

To my intense relief, that got through to her, and Nathan managed to coax Mrs Hansen to follow the gargoyles out of this section of the forest. As the last gargoyle departed, the other fairies withdrew into their houses before I could apologise for Steve's behaviour. Nathan cast a glance back before he departed, leaving me alone with my dad and Sky.

My cheeks burned with humiliation. "I'm sorry."

"You have nothing to be sorry for," Dad insisted.

"I hoped we'd be able to get through the first stage of introducing new fairies to town without any issues," I said. "A kid going missing in the woods is the sort of headline-making story that's going to set us back to square one."

"I know," he said. "I expected a visit from the gargoyles at some point, though. They've been looking for a reason to sow distrust towards the fairies, and I have no doubt some among the witch covens agree with them."

I hadn't known he'd been paying close attention, though he'd lived in the town before my birth when he'd been with my mother and had doubtless seen the witches' attitudes for himself.

"Some of them agreed with the hunters," I acknowledged. "And I guess they don't like admitting they were wrong. Even the ones who don't agree, though... the witches tend to gossip like nobody's business. Word will get around town, and the accusation alone will make people more likely to treat the fairies like outsiders."

"Most of us are used to it by now," he said mildly. "We know to be patient. Change is difficult for some."

No kidding. My own arrival in town had caused enough of a stir in itself, from the moment Nathan had ambushed me at the border as a suspected intruder after I'd accidentally wandered past the magical barriers preventing any ordinary folk from stumbling into town. We'd both come a long way since then, and this new challenge was only the latest I'd dealt with in the almost-a-year I'd lived in Fairy Falls.

"Where'd she even get those stories from?" I asked. "Fairies kidnapping human children, I mean. She seems to know an awful lot about it for someone whose daughter only disappeared today."

Mrs Hansen's shock at her daughter's disappearance

was understandable, but her attitude hadn't sprung up on its own, surely.

"There are folk tales even among the normals that concern the fairies," said Dad. "Tales of human children being taken and changelings left in their place, of trickery wrought upon humans by fairies they have wronged… and all tales have a kernel of truth in them."

I turned this information over in my mind, not sure I liked the implication. "I'm pretty sure none of the fairies here would have taken a human child captive, though."

"Of course not," he said, "but we cannot always control how others perceive us, especially when they have had centuries to form their opinions."

Didn't I know it. "Yeah. Steve didn't help by stomping around and scaring everyone, though he should know better. Did I mention he locked *me* in a cell?"

"That doesn't surprise me," said my dad. "He strikes me as the sort who enjoys exerting authority but not the other aspects of his position."

"Like dealing with the public," I said. "Even Steve doesn't want the hunters coming back, though. I hope that's enough for him to shut down Mrs Hansen's accusations."

"None of us want them back," said Dad. "Including Mrs Hansen, deep down."

I followed his gaze to the other fairies' houses. "Will they be okay?"

"Of course they will," he said. "They know they can speak to me or Conor if they have any concerns."

"Good," I said. "If that Mrs Hansen comes back, I don't want her ambushing anyone."

"She won't," he said. "Mostly because she won't be able

to find her way back to our part of the forest without following someone else."

"As long as she doesn't keep pestering Nathan," I said. "She seems to think he supports the hunters, which is ridiculous, but I wish... I wish their influence would go away."

"So do I, Blair," he said quietly. "They stole years of my life, but I'm infinitely grateful I can spend the rest of them with you."

Gratitude sprang up inside me, and I blinked a couple of times as he squeezed my shoulder with one hand. "Me too. See you later?"

"Yes. You should go and find Nathan," he said. "I know he wants to see you."

Yeah. He does. Since Nathan was the head of the town's security and worked long and unpredictable hours, we had enough trouble getting our schedules to match up without adding my new project of welcoming the new fairies to town in my spare time. Of which I had little. My dad had yet to start mingling with the other paranormals or find a job in town, so he had a lot of free time, but where his money came from, I wasn't entirely sure. Maybe it came from being a prince. I'd never asked, but I wasn't about to complain about him living close to me.

After parting ways with my dad, I retraced my steps down the path that led to the regular part of the forest and tracked the gargoyles by the sound of their wings bashing against trees and causing leaves to shower onto our heads. I then pinpointed Nathan, who'd managed to shake off his pursuer by concealing himself amid a particularly thick patch of trees.

Spotting me, he arched a brow in surprise. "You okay,

Blair? I thought you were staying with the fairies for a bit."

"I'm good," I said. "I think the fairies want some time alone to settle into their new home. Have you found her yet?"

"No, but the gargoyles will have turned this place inside out within the hour," he said. "Did your dad tell you to come and find me?"

I gave a slight smile. "He knows you're always working. We're rarely in the same place for long."

I'd blame Steve for that one, but Nathan had taken on a fair bit of responsibility of his own free will when he'd taken over the town's security team. Even after adding his sister Erin and her fiancé, Buck, he still bore most of the responsibility himself, on top of tolerating people like Mrs Hansen pestering him.

"True," he said, sliding his hand into mine. "Truth be told, I'm off duty at the moment. If I could fly above the forest, I'd be able to help with the search."

"Wings can only get you so far."

On cue, Ink Face's giant leathery wing became wedged in the canopy, causing him to come to an abrupt halt in mid-flight. As he kicked and flailed around, resembling a lopsided and rather ugly Christmas decoration, I burst into stifled giggles.

Nathan and I backed into the bushes before our laughter drew the irate gargoyle's attention.

"The girl will turn up, right?" I said to Nathan. "She can't go far through the woods without wandering into the elves' territory or the werewolves', and they'll return her to her mother right away."

Nathan squeezed my hand in reassurance. "Hopefully before her mother can cause too much of a fuss."

I grimaced, imagining her stomping around the forest all night. "I bet you're glad not to be on the evening shift."

"At least if I was, I could keep an eye out for her."

"She wouldn't have made it all the way to the town's border, though," I said. "Would she?"

"Unlikely." He glanced at me. "We'll search until dusk. Afterwards, are you free to come with me to the Troll's Tavern?"

"It's a date." I smiled, but a pang hit me, thinking of the fairies, who'd had their first taste of Steve's erratic policing methods as well as hostility from the residents.

The idea of a young child wandering around the woods at night wasn't appealing, either, but the werewolves were always on the lookout for trespassers, and the elves would be sure to return her to her parents if they found her. All the same, this was not an auspicious beginning to the new fairies' introduction to our town.

3

At work the following day, Laurel's disappearance lurked in the back of my mind despite my best efforts. Nathan and I had helped with the search until the darkness hindered our efforts, at which point he'd asked the night patrol to keep an eye out for her. I'd little doubt he'd be out there himself first thing in the morning and had not been surprised to wake up to find him gone.

I, however, had to focus on my regular job, which meant another day of trying to find employment for the two fairies who'd recently moved to town. On paper, their qualifications were pristine, but a significant number of employers required applicants to be able to use a wand, and fairies didn't typically need one in order to use magic. I scowled at the paper as I ticked yet another potential employer off the list.

Since the Inquisitor's departure and my dad's freedom, I'd been doing my best to reach out to more fairy clients for Dritch & Co. If they applied for jobs in Fairy Falls, they'd have a natural reason to move here and would have less trouble fitting in… if I found a way around the pesky wand requirement, that was.

Bethan sat at my side, going through paperwork at a dizzying rate as usual. Across from both of us sat Lizzie, who'd built the printer and coffee machine and whose bright-pink-painted nails raced across the keyboard as she answered emails. Then there was Rob, the cheerful blond werewolf who handled all our most difficult clients and supplied everyone with coffee when necessary.

He raised a brow at me across the table. "What's up, Blair? You've been staring at that page for a good five minutes now."

"Trying to find a good entry-level job that doesn't require a wand." I put down the page. "What's with that requirement, anyway? You shouldn't need a wand to stack shelves or wait tables."

A rare scowl crossed his face. "Usually a ploy to keep werewolves and other paranormals from applying."

"And fairies." I picked up the page again. "There's got to be some kind of rule against that."

"You'd think," said Rob. "Makes it easier to pick where *not* to apply, though. I like it when small-minded people advertise themselves up front. Coffee?"

"Please." I rubbed my temples while he ambled over to the coffee machine to bring me my caffeine fix. "Did you ever try applying for jobs outside of Fairy Falls?"

"A few," he said. "Never got asked to an interview. My first job was carrying equipment for the pack's band."

"Rather you than me." I suppressed a shudder at the memory of the werewolf-only band that put on a 'show' at their local pub on a nightly basis and didn't care if their musical prowess left much to be desired.

He deposited my coffee on the desk. "Yeah, I got out of that one pretty quickly. The chief wasn't pleased when I applied here, but I think he's glad I stuck close to the pack."

"And we're glad to have you to bring us coffee." I picked up my mug and took a long sip.

"Speaking of the chief," he said, "he's been giving us grief about that girl who disappeared in the forest yesterday."

I choked on my coffee and put down the mug. "They still haven't found her?"

"Not according to Chief Donovan," he said. "He told us to keep an eye out in case she wanders onto our territory, so everyone's on high alert."

"Ah." I'd figured the werewolf chief would have words to say about the situation given his prickliness at the notion of anyone encroaching on his territory. "Yeah, I doubt she'll wander that far north in the woods. I think she's more likely to stumble across the fairies or elves first."

"Yeah… about that," he said. "Chief Donovan's also not happy about the fairies living in the forest. Says that if they take any more of the witches' territory, they'll come after ours instead."

That figured. "He does know they aren't taking up any space, doesn't he? Fairy glamour can create a kind of bubble universe separate from ours that doesn't overlap with the real forest. I'm pretty sure there's no limit on its size."

Rob blinked. "That's… weird. No offence."

"Any weirder than shifting into a wolf?"

Too late, I realised the others had started listening in. Specifically Veronica, the boss, who'd just entered the office and was watching the pair of us from the doorway.

Veronica, who had her daughter's tall, lean frame and pale skin but had white hair instead of black, sauntered over to my desk and dropped off more paperwork between Bethan and me. "Working hard, everyone?"

"Yes, but I'm having a slight issue." I held up the list of employers. "I'm having trouble finding employers who are willing to hire people who can't use a wand."

"Ah." She eyed the paper. "How vexing. Yes, I can see how that'd make things tricky."

To Veronica, 'vexing' covered everything from minor client difficulties to a dead body in the office. "Is there a way I can filter out the ones that aren't any use?"

"I'm afraid we don't have that feature in our databases yet," she said. "You're welcome to start one yourself, of course."

Translation: I was on my own. Oh, well. Maybe I'd save a future employee some hassle if I put together a database of employers suitable for our fairy clients. "Okay, I can do that."

Veronica hovered beside my desk. "As long as there aren't any other problems, Blair?"

"No," I said. "None whatsoever."

My boss was well aware of the trials and tribulations I'd faced in the last few months, and she'd even helped me get through my conflict with the Inquisitor in one piece. Compared to that, helping the fairies would be a breeze, right?

The printer made noises in the corner as if to rebuke

me for lying to the boss, which I did my best to ignore. It wasn't as if I could do anything to find the missing girl while I was at work, and besides, the police or the forest's inhabitants were more likely to be able to track her down. I'd just have to be patient like everyone else.

Sorting the list of employers into 'wands' and 'no wands' was slow, tedious work, but it took my mind off my mild annoyance at Rob. He hadn't meant to insult me, but his words were a reminder that the fairies were out of step with the paranormal world at large and that Mrs Hansen's accusations were only one symptom of the issue.

Then again, look at the enmity between the were-wolves and the vampires or the witches and the elves. In fact, I wasn't convinced the majority of the local werewolf pack liked any other paranormals at all, and the chief had kicked up a huge fuss when two of his family members had ended up working here at Dritch & Co. In the end, though, he'd had to accept their choice. I hoped the same would be true of those with reservations about the fairies.

After work, I headed to the witches' headquarters for today's magic lesson. Rita, my tutor, also taught Rebecca, the new Head Witch. We were both on the level of the average nine-year-old, though since Rebecca was eleven, that was slightly less humiliating for her than it was for me. Admittedly, since she was also Head Witch and the holder of the sceptre, she had to deal with a level of pressure that none of the rest of us did.

Regardless, she'd been growing more confident in recent weeks as a result of the absence of her scheming mother and the support of her familiar, Toast. The large orange cat had been her steadiest ally since she'd adopted him, and he always meowed encouragement at her during our lessons. Sky, on the other hand, only showed up for familiar training lessons, and he made a point of avoiding me whenever I had a wand in my hand. When he did show his face for theory classes, he tended to fall asleep under the desk, like he had now. In fairness, I could relate, so I let him snooze on my feet as I watched Rita stand at the front of the classroom.

"Today, we'll be learning about the covens' history," said Rita, a forty-something witch who wore a large number of bangles that clacked together whenever she moved. "I thought that was an appropriate topic."

"You mean the local ones?" I asked.

"Of course." She cleared her throat and read from the textbook in front of her. "The witches were the first para-normals to come and live in Fairy Falls, where they founded the first covens..."

Too late, it dawned on me that she was talking about my ancestors—who'd founded the local covens, and they'd driven out the fairies in order to do it. I struggled to keep my knowledge of the true history out of my mind as she read on, but when no mention of the fairies showed up, my fidgeting grew notable enough to annoy Sky into waking up, at which point he grumpily prodded me in the ankle until I stifled a yelp.

"Yes, Blair?" said Rita, seeing me fidgeting. "Is there something you wanted to ask?"

I shuffled my seat back out of range of my cat's claws. "Um, Rita, have they considered updating the textbooks to include the banishment of the fairies from the Falls?"

Her brow wrinkled. "Considering that information isn't widely available and that the author of this textbook died some decades back, that would be difficult."

"But—then shouldn't it be updated?" I asked. "It's recent history."

"You'll have to ask Madame Grey," said Rita. "I'm afraid we don't write the curriculum textbooks ourselves, and besides, unless you raise the issue with the witches in charge of the academy's syllabus, you aren't likely to get very far. I'm sorry."

I found myself regretting bringing up the subject, but I did wonder what would happen if the fairies grew numerous enough to want to integrate into the witches' schools and universities and were then confronted by hearing a censored version of their history. I doubted they'd be thrilled at their exclusion.

"Okay," I said. "Never mind."

I passed the rest of the lesson in subdued silence while Sky returned to napping at my feet. Rebecca cast a few sympathetic looks in my direction, but since there was nothing either of us could do, I settled for daydreaming about writing about the fairies in my third-level examination and hoping the witches who'd have to mark my essay didn't object.

After our lesson ended, I went home and unlocked the door to the ground-floor flat I shared with Alissa, Madame Grey's granddaughter. In the living room, Alissa waved at me from the sofa. "Hey, Blair."

"Hey." Sky raced ahead of me to our spot on the sofa, while the pixie zipped over my shoulder, making loud chittering noises. For some reason, he still liked hanging around our flat despite the growing number of pixies moving to the fairies' part of the forest. "No shift today?"

"Nah, but I'm working early tomorrow," she said.

"Samuel and I went out hiking today. How was your magic lesson?"

"Not too bad." I sat on the sofa and scratched Sky behind the ears. "I think Rita is trying to hurry our lessons along to help us catch up to the others. More Rebecca than me."

"Yeah, I understand that," she said. "Being Head Witch is a lot of pressure. Madame Grey said she wants to take her to meet more of the other witches in the other regions too."

"Yeah, as long as it doesn't clash with her schoolwork," I said. "I'm the one causing trouble at the moment, though. I... um, I kind of contradicted Rita over the textbook excluding the fairies from the story of the covens who founded the town."

"Ah," she said. "I guess it's hard to update the textbooks when the fairies haven't mingled with the witches for so many years. Most of us didn't have much of a clue until recently."

"Still, the covens have magic," I said. "Shouldn't that make it easier?"

"Magic can't do everything."

Didn't I know it. Even my lie-sensing power had its limits, which I'd been reminded of when I'd gone up against the Inquisitor. Admittedly, my skill at fairy magic was also lagging behind that of other fairies of my age, since most of my knowledge had come from the pixie and my cat. I'd been getting better at using glamour to change my appearance, but I wasn't sure if I'd ever be able to conjure up a lightning storm like Conor or make myself unidentifiable to other fairies like the Inquisitor did... not that I aspired to be anything like *him.*

Still, at least I had a chance at learning now that I'd re-established contact with my dad and the fairies were coming back to town, even if our efforts weren't progressing as quickly as I'd have liked. I'd even started Dritch & Co's first fairy-friendly database. That had to count for something, right?

My phone buzzed in my pocket, and I found my dad was calling me. He hadn't figured out texting yet, but that knowledge didn't quell my nervous reaction.

"Hey, Dad," I answered. "Everything okay?"

"Yes… we've got a lead on the missing girl," he said. "I wondered if you wanted to come and help."

"Oh," I said. "Um, sure."

"Good. I'll meet you by the forest."

The call ended. Alissa gave me a quizzical look, to which I responded, "Dad said there's a lead on the missing girl. Sky, do you want to come?"

"Miaow."

Taking that to mean 'yes,' I beckoned him to follow me as I went to retrieve my coat and shoes. Alissa watched me, stroking Roald, her familiar. "I didn't know you were investigating the girl's disappearance, Blair."

"She disappeared near the fairies' part of the woods," I explained. "Her mother… she's convinced the fairies kidnapped her, and she's been giving the police a lot of trouble. Nathan too. If she's come back, I don't want to leave my dad to face her alone."

"Oh, fun." She pulled a face. "I did wonder if you and Steve had had another altercation, considering you were in the forest at the time."

"Yeah, he's not happy with me for getting involved," I said. "But I've been helping the fairies move to town from the beginning. I'm not going to let him keep hassling them."

"Yeah," she said. "I only hope this is a one-off and the girl shows up soon. Samuel said he's been hearing things from a few people at the university…"

I frowned. "What kind of things?"

"Um, there's a group of people who've been meeting in the library to exchange rumours about the fairies." Despite her casual tone, Alissa's attention was on petting her cat rather than meeting my eyes. "It's nothing too serious, I don't think. Just a few rumours about the fairies being dangerous mischief makers. I'm sure the same thing must have happened when the university first opened to non-witches and wizards and started letting in shifters and other paranormals as well. I think when some of them come to the university, they'll be able to see for themselves that the fairies don't mean any harm."

I hoped she was right, but I didn't need to be distracted by worrying about the local students' attitudes to the newcomers when we had enough strife to handle with Mrs Hansen's stories about the fairies stealing human children.

"I hope you're right." I shrugged into my coat and left the flat with Sky padding at my heels.

When I reached the path that led into the forest near the Falls, I spotted my dad standing next to Conor, facing the lake. Neither of them noticed me at first.

"This isn't necessary," Conor was saying in a low voice.

"You know it is," said Dad. "If he doesn't show his face to the police, then they'll take it as an admission of guilt. You should have told me he was here."

"What's going on?" I asked.

"There's another fairy living in town." Dad turned around, displaying no surprise at the sight of me. "He's hidden beneath a glamour, which Conor knew about, but he decided not to mention it to me or to anyone else until now."

"What does that have to do with the missing girl?" I queried.

"Nothing whatsoever," said Conor. "You're making a fuss over nothing."

"I'm trying to anticipate any potential issues for you and the other fairies," he said. "If you want the police to leave you be, you need to abide by the laws."

"The laws." Conor scoffed. "It's none of my business if someone wants to seek solitude here."

"If they're living in Fairy Falls, then…" I faltered at his blistering look. "I'm not going to tell anyone what to do, but Steve will kick up a fuss if he finds out, and we don't want him to make it more difficult for the other fairies to move here."

"We were here first," Conor said. "As you'd do well to remember."

"Whoa." I raised my hands. "I don't want an argument, but don't forget a girl is missing somewhere in the forest, and everyone is bound to be more on edge than usual. Where is this other fairy, then?"

"We'll go and talk to him," said Dad. "I'm sure we can sort this out quickly enough."

Conor's scowl deepened, but he didn't say anything when Dad and I left the path and walked through the woods until he was out of earshot.

"Why would another fairy have moved here without introducing himself to the others?" I asked.

"Many fairies are loners," he said. "Those who've left the Courts especially. They isolated themselves for a reason."

"Yeah, I understand that," I said. "I doubt Steve would see it that way, though. Is he likely to kick up a fuss?"

"It depends on whether or not the fairy told the others of his presence here," he said. "If Steve finds out everyone knew except for him, it might get them into trouble too."

I grimaced. "Maybe I should call Nathan. He's the point of call between Steve and… everyone else."

The two had somewhat repaired their alliance after Nathan had inadvertently taken some responsibilities away from him and his fellow gargoyles by taking command of the town's security in order to keep the hunters out, and while I wouldn't exactly have called them friends, Nathan was one of the few people who stood a chance of convincing Steve not to toss the fairy out of town without listening for an explanation.

"Maybe, but it doesn't have to be Steve the newcomer introduces himself to," said Dad. "It's Madame Grey who keeps a register of everyone living in town, right? I can't promise the idea of *her* coming into the fairies' part of town will go down well, but that seems a better option than getting Steve involved."

I had to agree. Madame Grey was fairer than the gargoyles, and she'd be fine with hearing out the newcomer.

For now, I let my dad lead the way through the part of the forest that bordered the lake until we veered off the path and found ourselves in a clearing. In the centre, flanked by large oak trees, stood a large toadstool that I only realised was a house when I saw the windows and door cut out of its spotted edges. A little weird, but who was I to judge? "Is this the place?"

A fairy with long silver hair appeared in the doorway, his green eyes glowing like emeralds. "What do you want?"

"This is Oak," Dad told me. "Oak, this is Blair Wilkes, and I am her father, Braden Eventide."

"I know who you are," said the fairy. "You're the exiled prince."

I blinked in surprise. He didn't sound deferential like the other fairies did. In fact, his tone held an almost derisive note.

"And I'm his daughter," I said. "How long have you been living here?"

"I fail to see what concern it is to you," he said. "This is my home."

"Unfortunately, you're also within the limits of the town of Fairy Falls, which makes you a citizen," said Dad. "That means you need to tell Madame Grey of the Meadowsweet Coven you're here before someone stumbles upon your home by accident."

"A curse upon the covens," said Oak, his voice echoing around the clearing. The hairs on my arms stood on end as the air tingled with static. "They are the reason I must live in hiding. I will not speak to them."

"I'm not going to order you to introduce yourself to the other fairies," said Dad, "but I think it would make your life much easier if you told the authorities you are living here. It doesn't have to be the witches. You can speak to the police or the head of the security team instead."

I grimaced, knowing the fairy would not be impressed

with Nathan given his former hunter status. Or Erin and Buck, for that matter. "All you have to do is tell them you're living here and they'll leave you in peace."

The fairy's eyes narrowed in annoyance. "If you want to leave me in peace, why is everyone acting as though I'm a dangerous stray?"

"Because a human child disappeared in the woods yesterday, and her mother is blaming the fairies," I said. "I'm not accusing you of having anything to do with her disappearance, but everyone is on edge, and if the police find you here before you show your face, the other fairies will suffer the backlash as well."

The air shivered again, the grass around the toadstool-shaped house swaying in the breeze. "If they want to challenge me, then I'll remind the covens that they personally burned down my last home and drove me out of the forest."

Whoa. "How... how long ago was that?"

"Long enough ago for everyone in town to have forgotten," Dad said from my side. "Oak, the witches aren't the same as they were before."

No... but I had the sinking suspicion that he'd been referring to my own ancestors, who'd driven him and the other fairies out of town. I hadn't known anyone here in Fairy Falls had been alive all those years ago, much less that they had a clear recollection of the incident.

"I'm sorry for that." My words sounded hollow, but short of pulling out a time machine, there was nothing I could do to fix the damage. "I'm sure Madame Grey would agree too. She isn't from the same coven who drove you out. Nor is she old enough to remember."

"I'm aware of that, Blair *Wildflower*." The fairy sneered at me. "Get away from my house."

And with that, he slammed the door in my face. My heart thudded in response. "Dad… I think you should have come alone."

"It wouldn't have made a difference, Blair." He reached out and squeezed my shoulder in reassurance. "Don't forget I willingly turned my back on him and the others when I met Tanith."

Dizziness swept over me. "Wait, were you alive then too?"

"No." He paused for a heartbeat. "But I am older than I look, yes."

My throat closed up. "Am… am *I* immortal?"

I'd never given much thought to the matter, but if all fairies were immortal and humans weren't, where did that leave someone like me? I mean, Nathan was mortal, and so were my friends and co-workers. The idea of outliving them all did not appeal in the slightest. Okay, Alissa was dating an immortal vampire herself and hadn't mentioned if that'd created any issues between the pair of them, but still.

My dad squeezed my shoulder. "No. You didn't grow up in the fairy realm, and you're half-human, so you'll live a regular life span."

"That's good." I studied the closed door of Oak's house. "I think."

After all, if Oak's attitude was anything to go by, I'd always be an outsider to some, even among the fairies.

4

"You're being quiet, Blair," Erin commented.

From the seat next to mine, Nathan shot me a concerned look, which I returned with a false smile. Generally, Nathan's sister talked enough for the rest of us put together on our double dates with her and Buck at the Troll's Tavern anyway, yet hours after our conversation, I couldn't seem to shake Oak's words from my mind. Neither could I forget that I was technically breaking the law by not mentioning the town's secret new resident to Nathan or his sister. Though a crowded pub was definitely not the place to mention that a centuries-old fairy was hiding in a toadstool and railing against the covens.

"I was thinking about the missing girl," I said. "Didn't want to ruin the mood."

"Oh." Erin's face fell. "Yeah… we searched the woods for ages over the last couple of days. She must've found a good hiding place."

"Are you sure she's hiding?" asked Buck. "I know the

forest is huge, but everyone seems to know their particular corner of it pretty well, from what I've heard."

"What's the alternative?" said Erin. "The werewolves wouldn't have captured a human child. As for the elves or fairies… what would be the point?"

"I doubt she actually got kidnapped by fairies," I said, "but her mother seems to have the impression that's the case."

"Ouch," said Erin. "That's got to be rough on the newcomers."

"You're telling me." I stole a glance at Buck, wondering what he thought about all this. He was half-fairy, like me, though he usually wore his human guise and rarely took out his wings out of a habit of self-consciousness about his fairy appearance. "I'm sure she'll turn up, but it's hard to forget people are forming opinions about the fairies based on this."

"Then that's their problem," said Erin firmly. "Forget them."

"Exactly," said Buck. "I'm sure they're in the minority."

I hope. Oak sprang to mind once again, since he was all but proving their point about the fairies' untrustworthy natures. While I needed to confide in someone, Erin was notorious for gossiping, and if the fairy found out everyone in town knew of his presence, he'd be even less inclined to play along. On the other hand…

I waited until the meal was over before I waylaid Buck on the way out of the restaurant. "Buck, can I have a word?"

He caught my eye, surprise crossing his face. "Sure."

We waited for the others to overtake us before I spoke to him. "I know you have enough going on, but I found out today that there's a fairy living in town who refuses to introduce himself to the coven or the police. I wondered if you might be able to talk to him, since you're new to town too."

His own meeting with Madame Grey had been quick and without any problems, but he'd already had a job working for Nathan's security team and was also half human and had been living in the human realm for his entire life. Oak, though, saw himself as an outsider and did not seem at all interested in changing that fact.

"Another fairy?" he said. "I guess I can pay him a visit when I have the time."

"He's also a cranky centuries-old immortal who blames the witches for driving him out of town... in person," I added. "Just so you know."

He whistled. "He's that old? Really?"

"Apparently so," I said. "I'd rather not have Steve find him first and throw a fit, so it'd be appreciated if you didn't tell anyone, even Erin."

"I'll keep it quiet," he said. "Give me a shout when you need me."

"Tomorrow after work would be the best time." I didn't have a magic lesson tomorrow. They tended to vary depending on Rita's schedule—and Rebecca's too. "That okay?"

Erin turned back and shot both of us a curious look, but Buck nodded, readying himself to catch up to her. "Sure. See you then."

As he caught up to Erin, I rejoined Nathan, hoping that Buck's presence would persuade Oak to soften his attitude a little. As long as he didn't figure out Buck had a past as a hunter, of course. That might cause issues. Then again, for all I knew, Oak was a secret supporter of the Inquisitor. It wouldn't be the first time I'd met a fairy who'd wanted the hunters to push the covens out of power. We'd managed to bring the fairies back to town without the hunters needing to take power, of course, but some had seen capitulating to the hunters as the only way to reclaim the town they'd lost so long ago.

Whatever the case, I hoped Buck would be able to get through to him where my dad and I had failed.

———

As planned, I met Buck outside work the following day. The blond half fairy was still in his human guise when I left Dritch & Co's office, glancing furtively around him as if he'd expected to be followed.

"You know how hard it was to shake Erin off?" he said. "I figured I'd pretend I'd been called out to an urgent patrol to have an excuse to run out alone, but she insisted on checking the schedule and ruining the ruse. I sneaked out of the house while she was in the shower instead."

"Sorry about all the secrecy," I said. "It's also probably better if I don't go near Oak's house when you're there too. He's a little jumpy."

"You're really not selling this to me," he said. "If I disappear in the forest, Erin will storm in there and raise a fuss that will make the gargoyles look halfway reasonable."

"I'm just nervous," I admitted. "Not so much about him but about how the others will react when they find out he's been hiding in plain sight. There are a few people who are being less than welcoming to the newcomers already. I can't believe that girl hasn't shown up yet either."

"Yeah, that probably isn't helping."

We walked towards the lake and the forest together, at which point it occurred to me that I hadn't memorised the way to Oak's house. Buck gave me an eye roll when I walked straight into a swathe of undergrowth instead. "Are you sure this fairy hasn't already taken off in the night like the goblin market?"

"He's here somewhere." I listened, hearing the distant sound of voices from somewhere among the trees. "That's not him, though."

Buck's head turned in that direction too. "Something going on over there?"

My heart sank when I recognised Mrs Hansen's voice among the shouts. "I'd say there is."

"Sounds like trouble," Buck said. "Which means it's my business."

The two of us made our way towards the sound of angry voices, which turned out to be coming from the area of the forest near the other fairies' home. When we rounded a corner, we found several fairies had gathered opposite a group of witches and wizards, some of whom were holding handmade signs. The wizard at the front of the group was a youth with a buzz cut and a giant sign in his hands that read No Feeries. While the spelling made me worry for the standards of the academy's lessons, he also carried a bright flower in his pocket, which confused me until I recognised its purple hue. *Those flowers are deadly to fairies.*

He had some nerve carrying anti-fairy poison in the fairies' own part of the forest, but before I could say a word, Mrs Hansen moved to the centre of their group, an expression of angry defiance on her face.

"What is going on?" said Buck, correctly identifying her as the instigator of the trouble.

"These people are causing a disturbance," said one of the fairies. "They've been standing outside our homes and yelling for the past half hour."

"My daughter is missing," Mrs Hansen said in shrill tones. "She's been gone for days. I won't stand for your lies any longer, and if the police won't do anything about you, then I will."

"Bothering people who had nothing to do with her disappearance won't do anything to bring your daughter back," I told her.

"They had everything to do with her disappearance." Mrs Hansen wheeled around to glare at me.

"That's enough," said Buck. "Unless you have a reason to be here, then all of you need to leave. That includes you, Mrs Hansen."

The others didn't like that a bit. They bristled and grumbled among themselves and waved their posters threateningly.

"I'll do no such thing." Mrs Hansen directed her attention at Buck instead. "You've seen what these freaks are capable of, haven't you? You know they're dangerous."

She thought Buck was an active hunter too? I almost wanted him to get his wings out just to see the look on her face, but instead, he said, "I'm going to ask you to leave before I call the police."

Mrs Hansen puffed up like a frog, her face flushing. Fortunately, at that moment, my dad appeared from the bushes, striding over to the gathering humans. Though they doubtless neither knew nor cared that he'd once been a prince, his regal demeanour was visible even to humans, because the others stopped voicing complaints at once.

"I would advise you all to leave before we call the authorities," he said. "You shouldn't be here."

"Neither should you," said the shaven-headed dude. "Your people are kidnapping human children."

"You're mistaken," Dad said. "You aren't achieving anything by harassing the inhabitants of the forest. Leave."

This time, Mrs Hansen did look a little cowed. Maybe it was the subtle aura of authority my dad gave off, which reminded me of Madame Grey in a way. In any case, it worked, and the group of strangers sloped away, posters and all—except for Mrs Hansen, who waited until my dad gave her another warning look before striding off after the others. A moment later, the fairies themselves dispersed into the trees.

"I'm guessing those were the kids from the university Samuel mentioned?" I murmured. "The ones campaigning against the fairies?"

"Don't ask me," said Buck. "I didn't know there was anyone at the university who was campaigning against the newcomers."

"According to Alissa," I said. "That guy looked like trouble. Is it even legal for him to carry that flower around in the forest?"

"Technically, but it shouldn't be used to threaten the fairies." My dad walked over to my side. "I'll have to talk to the covens, I think."

"Yeah, Madame Grey should know about this," I said.

"I heard a few kids at the university were spreading rumours about the fairies but not that they'd organised themselves into a team. Or recruited Mrs Hansen."

"They're flocking around her because her child's disappearance provides them with a convenient example to use against the fairies," he said. "She'll realise they're using her soon enough, and she'll stop associating with them in the end. Mark my words."

"I hope you're right," I said. "I can't believe that guy had the nerve to come in here and raise a fuss. It's lucky the fairies aren't as territorial as the elves are."

"Some are," Dad said, eyeing Buck. "Have we met before?"

"Ah, this is Buck," I said. "He's a half fairy like me, and I asked him to convince Oak to introduce himself to the witches."

I'd forgotten the two had yet to meet. Dad had met Nathan and Erin, of course, but he generally kept his distance from the town's security team. Smart idea given the gargoyles' previous links to the hunters.

"Whereabouts does this Oak live?" Buck scanned the place where the fairies had disappeared, confusion rippling across his face as he took in the path that was half-visible, half not.

"I'll take you there," said Dad. "I've left him alone since our last encounter. I hope he'll be amenable to talking to you."

Buck looked even less convinced than he had previously, but he nodded. "Okay."

My dad took the lead, which came as a relief, because it turned out I'd been leading Buck in completely the wrong direction. When we reached the path that led to

Oak's odd toadstool-shaped home, my dad and I halted behind a patch of trees so he wouldn't look out the window and spot us.

Buck squinted at the house. "That's… different. I have to go there alone?"

"He hates my family," I said. "I wouldn't ask you to do this if I had another choice, but…"

"But you don't. I know." Buck nodded. "All right. But you owe me one for this."

"No worries," I said. "I'd just rather get this over with before Mrs Hansen and her friends find him first and report him to the police."

"Fair enough." He walked towards the toadstool-shaped house, his shoulders set in determination.

My dad and I stepped back out of view of the door— and a moment later, the ground gave way beneath Buck's feet. He fell with a startled cry into a hole that hadn't been there before and vanished from sight.

"Buck!" I hadn't intended to reveal myself in front of Oak, but I couldn't leave Buck in whatever trap he'd fallen into. I ran over and found Buck sprawled at the bottom of a deep hole in the ground, too deep for me to reach in and pull him out.

I leaned over the edge and then remembered my wings. *Way to forget the obvious, Blair.* Sliding awkwardly over the edge, I lowered myself into the hole in the ground, beating my wings to keep from falling. I caught up with Buck at the bottom, who lay tangled in some kind of net that I couldn't see clearly in the lack of sunlight.

"Blair, what are you doing?" He tried to move back to give me more room, but the lack of space made it difficult.

"This isn't a hunters' net, is it?" I didn't think so. If it had been, I'd have been ensnared myself. "How can I get you out of there?"

"You can start by not treading on my foot," he said dryly.

"Sorry!" I shuffled to the side, realising belatedly that I'd accidentally entangled my own feet in the net when I'd landed. Knots of rope caught on my shoes, and when I tugged on them, Buck stumbled back into the wall.

"Wait." He grunted, trying to pull his leg free. The movement yanked me onto my rear, further entangling the pair of us. "Blair, don't move."

"Little hard not to." I suppressed an inexplicable laugh. "This is a fine mess we've landed in, isn't it? What would Erin think of you and I getting tangled in a net together?"

"She'd probably stand there and laugh at us." Buck struggled against the wall and snapped his fingers, revealing his own wings. "Might be easier if we fly out first."

"Hang on." When I shuffled to my feet, I noticed a flickering around the web-like net that hadn't been obvious before. It didn't seem to have a beginning or end, while its glow reminded me of Buck's glittering wings. "I think it might be an illusion. The net, I mean."

"Looks real to me," Buck remarked. "Feels real too."

"Glamour's like that." I took a piece of the net in my hand, willing my second sight to see through the illusion, and the flickering intensified. Then I snapped my fingers. At once, the entire net vanished from sight, leaving the pair of us alone in the pit.

"Nicely done," said Buck. "I take back the part about you owing me a favour."

"Good, because I don't think our friend up there wants

visitors." I peered up at the rim of the hole. "Let's get out of here."

"You first," he said. "We can't fly at the same time. There's not enough space."

"All right." I took flight in a couple of wingbeats and launched myself out of the hole… crashing straight into Oak.

Or I would have, but the fairy sprang back in a catlike motion that turned him into a blur before my eyes, while I caught my balance on the edge of the pit.

"You!" the fairy said, jabbing a finger at me. "You're trespassing."

"You trapped my friend in a spell," I said. "Both of us, in fact."

Buck emerged from the hole in a beating of wings. "I could accuse you of trespassing yourself, but I'm supposed to be here to welcome you to town."

"I don't live in your town," Oak retaliated. "I live here in the forest."

I pressed my fingers to my forehead, fighting a groan of frustration. "The forest is part of Fairy Falls, which you know perfectly well if you've lived here as long as you claim. Besides, Buck here moved to Fairy Falls a few weeks ago, and he settled in right away."

"That's right," said Buck. "Oak, is it? Some of us are capable of welcoming visitors without setting booby traps, you know."

"Let me guess: you've spent your life pretending to be human, like her?" The fairy's lip curled. "I have lived for too long to play along with pathetic human games."

"For someone supposed to be centuries old, you're acting like a toddler," said Buck. "All we want you to do is to introduce yourself to the local coven leaders. They don't bite."

"My magic does," he said.

This was going well. "Oak, either you can take the initiative or expect to wake up to find the police on your doorstep when they figure out you're living here without telling anyone. There's a human girl missing in the area and a group of angry protesters marching around, trying to pressure the covens into kicking you all out of town, as it is, so it's only a matter of time before someone finds you who isn't as friendly as we are."

The air around the fairy crackled with static. "I'd like to see them try."

"That is enough." My dad stepped into view. I'd been starting to wonder where he'd disappeared to. "If you wish to be left alone, I'd suggest you comply with the laws."

In answer, Oak returned to his house and slammed the door. I winced, staring at the wooden surface for an instant. "I guess he's not coming to meet the witches, then."

5

Our failed attempt to get Oak to cooperate hung over my head throughout the evening and during work the following day. It didn't help that all my attempts to arrange interviews for fairy clients were overshadowed by worry about what would happen if they arrived in town to Mrs Hansen and her allies waving banners telling them to go away.

My database for employers who accepted applications from those without wands was growing, though more slowly than I'd have liked, but I had yet to secure any interviews for Ani or Rosalyn. It didn't help that the employers who *didn't* have the wand requirement also required endless years of experience. I was pretty sure even most non-fairies would have struggled to meet that requirement. I debated getting the pair of them into the town's security team to join Buck and the others instead, but I wouldn't expect them to want to work in close proximity to Steve or the other gargoyles. Especially at a time like this.

As for Oak, I doubted *he* wanted me to find him employment, but my new database did not yet have a category for cranky immortals with zero understanding or care for following the rules. I trusted that Buck would keep quiet about the newcomer, but if Oak kept attacking anyone who went near his part of the forest, it was only a matter of time before someone noticed. Someone like Mrs Hansen, for instance.

After work, I left the office and stopped short at the sight of the pixie fluttering in front of the automatic doors, making agitated chittering noises.

"What is it?" In response, he flew in circles, beckoning me with one twig-like hand. "You want me to come with you?"

Crossing my fingers behind my back that Oak or Mrs Hansen hadn't started causing trouble again, I followed him along the street. Part of me expected him to lead me into the forest, but instead, he flew uphill through the middle of town and then kept going. When the town's distant border, which bridged the forest, came within sight, I realised he was leading me to the campus of the town's sole university. "Are those students up to something again?"

The pixie circled me in answer, beckoning me forward. I reached the gates, and my heart stuttered to a halt. On the fence circling the campus, someone had affixed a large poster with a drawing of what I assumed was supposed to be a fairy, with exaggerated pointed ears and wings. In its arms was a struggling human child wearing an expression of terror on its face. Several similar posters had been stuck to the walls of the campus buildings on the other side of the fence.

"Oh, no." I reached out and pulled the poster down in one swift motion, but to remove the others, I'd need to go into the campus itself. Bringing out my wings with a snap of my fingers, I rolled up the poster and tucked it under my arm before picking an inconspicuous point to hop over the fence.

My feet crashed into something solid but invisible, sending me rolling head over heels and catching my balance against the fence. My vision flickered, showing me a couple of fairies hidden beneath an illusion of a wall: Ani and Rosalyn, wearing glamour and watching the campus from behind their illusion.

"What are you doing?" I whispered.

"How'd you find us?" said Rosalyn.

"I can see through glamour," I reminded them. "Why are you hiding back here?"

Rosalyn straightened upright and snapped her fingers. Out of nowhere, a cloud of glitter rained down on the heads of a group of passing students. They ran, shrieking and trying to bat the glitter out of their hair.

"You're pranking the students?" I said.

"They came to our homes to intimidate us," said Rosalyn. "I think we're justified in having a bit of fun with them."

"You can just remove the posters instead," I suggested. "I don't like them, either, but the people you're hitting with glitter aren't the ones who were threatening you."

"They all allowed this," Ani pointed out. "Otherwise, someone else would have removed them."

I opened and closed my mouth, unable to disagree. "I doubt throwing glitter at them will help."

"It's better than nothing," Rosalyn said firmly.

I rose to my feet. "Tell you what, I'll talk to Samuel. He's a vampire who works at the library here. I'm sure he'll be willing to remove the posters."

Both of them looked sceptical, but they hadn't met Samuel, and I was sure he would be willing to listen. He knew *me*, after all.

Hoping the two fairies didn't try any more pranks on the students while I wasn't watching them, I made my way through the campus, which consisted of a maze of brick buildings decorated with motifs of dragons and unicorns and so many posters that it was no wonder the anti-fairy ones had gone largely unnoticed.

I'd memorised the way to the library, so I only took three wrong turnings before I found my way there. Inside the building, I found Samuel standing near the front of the circling rows of towering shelves that filled the room in a maze that rivalled the campus itself. I often wondered if it was built that way to make it impossible to steal any of the books. Or to make life more exciting for the vampire librarian, perhaps. His white fangs stood out against his dark skin as he greeted me with a smile.

"Ah, Blair," said Samuel. "Looking for more resources on fairy magic?"

"Not exactly." I showed him the rolled-up poster. "I'm looking for the reason these are suddenly all over campus."

Annoyance flickered in his eyes. "Yes, they appeared overnight. Rather shoddy artistry, in my opinion."

"Do you know *who* put them there?" I queried. "A wizard who happens to be a student here, perhaps?"

"You talked to Alissa."

"I also ran into a group of students protesting in the

woods," I said. "Led by a gormless-looking guy with a shaved head who seems to have a spelling problem."

"Rodney Ackers," said the vampire in disapproving tones. "He's rather notorious around here. I've thrown him out of the library at least once for causing a ruckus."

"Is his attitude a common one?" I queried. "Because I'm having second thoughts about encouraging fairies to apply to study here if they're going to be met with an angry mob."

"Certainly *not*," said the vampire. "I've read the minds of everyone who comes into my library, and very few want the fairies to be treated any differently than any other paranormals who come here. It's just unfortunate that this particular group have decided to start broadcasting their lies."

"So the posters are allowed, then?" I asked.

"As of yet, there isn't a rule against decorating the buildings," he said. "I intend to speak to the other staff, but it might take a while to convince them that the images of fairies are inappropriate."

"Or someone could just go and remove them," I added. "Nobody would notice, right?"

"Not if they were discreet enough."

"Good." Satisfied, I made for the door. "Thanks, Samuel."

When I left the library, I retraced my steps through the winding buildings and found the two fairies still hovering near the fence behind their illusory wall.

"Let me guess: you were unsuccessful," said Rosalyn.

"Getting the posters down the official way will take too long," I replied. "So... who wants to see how many posters we can remove without being noticed?"

Ani gave me a sceptical look. "This isn't allowed, is it?"

"Neither is throwing glitter at people." I snapped my fingers to glamour myself unseen and took flight. "Whoever gets the most posters down wins."

"Wins what?" Rosalyn said, interest in her tone.

"I'll think of something." Relief flooded me when they exchanged mischievous looks and then glamoured themselves unseen before taking off in a flutter of wings.

I flew towards the nearest poster, grabbing it with both hands and yanking it down. With my glamour in place, it was easy to evade watchful eyes as I removed the posters from the walls one by one. This struck me as a temporary measure, because as long as the rumours about the fairies' involvement in Laurel Hansen's disappearance persisted, it'd be hard to prevent Rodney Ackers and his friends from spreading lies around campus.

Maybe it would help if the town's true history was more widely known, but I wasn't convinced the witches would be able to do that by themselves. After all, the only survivors from the time were fairies, not witches. Like Oak. The notion of *him* coming to campus to set the record straight was a mildly terrifying one, I wouldn't lie.

After circling the campus twice and finding no tasteless fairy posters remaining, I returned to our former spot beside the fence, snapping my fingers to undo my glamour and waiting for the others to return.

After a moment, Ani and Rosalyn flew into view from different directions, depositing their hauls. They proceeded to count out their stolen posters with eagerness.

"I win," Rosalyn announced.

"No, Blair does," Ani responded. "She has one more

underneath that pile. See?"

I smiled, showing them my haul. "As the winner, I'm going to suggest we leave campus alone and go and get rid of these posters. Shred them to ribbons if you like, but no more pranks on the students. Deal?"

"Sure." Ani followed me over the fence without a fuss, followed by Rosalyn. I had to admit it felt pretty satisfying to leave campus with armfuls of posters and then find a private spot to shred them to pieces with our bare hands.

I was on my way back from dumping the shredded bits of paper in the nearest recycling bin when I spotted the large shape of a blond werewolf wandering around near the forest. I halted in my tracks then recognised him as Rob.

"Oh, hey, Blair," he said. "What're you doing out here?"

"Visiting campus," I replied. "Are you meeting someone?"

"Nah, I'm trying to get away from the chief," he replied. "He's in one of his moods because of those witches crashing around the forest, making a noise."

"Not Mrs Hansen again?" I said.

"Yeah, she's still insisting on looking for her missing daughter in person," he said. "She made the mistake of falling into a badger shifter's den earlier. It didn't end well for her."

Oh, no. "Wait, why is she on the shifters' territory? Did she find any clues over there?"

"No, she just has no sense of direction," he said. "I had to show her the way back to the witches' part of the forest, and I'm pretty sure she wound up near the elves' territory instead."

"I doubt their king would be pleased if she wandered

into their home."

The elves who chose to live in the forest were even more territorial than most fairies I'd met, and they had a tendency to wave weapons in the faces of anyone who got too close to their king. I hoped Mrs Hansen didn't make that mistake, because she didn't strike me as likely to be able to tell the difference between the elves and the fairies, and I doubted she was in the best of moods after her mishap in the badger shifter's den.

At that moment, Ani and Rosalyn caught up with me, eyeing the werewolf in confusion.

"What's going on?" asked Ani.

"Our human troublemaker is back in the forest," I explained. "Falling into shifter dens and pestering the elves."

Rosalyn's expression darkened. "Say… the *elves* didn't take her child, did they?"

"Maybe they did," said Ani. "They might have taken her so that we'd take the blame. They don't like us being near their territory any more than the witches do."

"Less, if anything," said Rosalyn.

"Hang on a second," I said hastily, conscious of Rob hovering awkwardly in the background. "Let's not jump to conclusions. I'm a friend of the Elf King, and he helped my dad hide from the hunters when he was on the run."

Ani looked mollified, but Rosalyn said, "Doesn't mean Mrs Hansen won't blame them anyway."

"Yeah… I should go and find her before she starts a fight," I said.

"Sure you don't want company?" asked Rob.

"I'd better not." After my disastrous attempt to get Buck to help me persuade Oak to come and talk to

Madame Grey, I figured I ought to stop dragging my friends into my weird fairy life. "I appreciate the offer, though. See you tomorrow?"

"See you at work." He waved me off, and I walked away from campus with the other two fairies.

The quickest way to reach the elves' section of the woods was via the entrance near the witches' part of town… which, unfortunately, happened to be close to Mrs Hansen's house and the place where Laurel had gone missing.

We turned down the road near the forest, which I belatedly remembered also happened to be where Annabel the seer's granddaughter lived with her elf husband in a pretty cottage that bordered the forest. I hadn't realised Mrs Hansen lived on the same street, but it immediately became clear which house was hers. Bright-purple flowers bloomed at every corner, growing up the walls of the cottage so that it resembled a giant bruise. A giant *fairy-proofed* bruise.

"Whoa," I said. "Someone's obsessed."

"No surprise," Ani said in distasteful tones. "We should tear them down."

"I wouldn't touch them," I warned. "Those things are lethal to fairies. Besides, it won't help matters if we mess with her house when she's not here."

The path into the woods was fortunately flower free, but it wasn't long before I heard shouting coming from farther up the path. My heart sank, and the other two fairies stopped glaring at Mrs Hansen's house to follow me into the woods.

We walked down the winding path in pursuit of the sound of Mrs Hansen's voice. It wasn't hard to pinpoint her location, so I tracked her down in a clearing, where she stood surrounded by a circle of elves. The elves were each around four feet tall with pointed ears and dressed in green-and-brown attire that blended with the surrounding forest... and all of them pointed sharpened branches straight at Mrs Hansen.

"Hang on!" I addressed Bramble, an elf I'd been acquainted with for a while. "What are you doing?"

"This witch came onto our territory and started threatening us," he said. "We simply returned the favour."

Oh, boy. "Her daughter disappeared in the forest the other day, and she's really worried about her, so she's not acting rationally. Mrs Hansen, come with me. You're going to leave the elves alone, right?"

"I most certainly am not!" Mrs Hansen said in shrill tones. "They kidnapped my child."

"I thought you blamed the fairies, not the elves."

A mistake. She spun on me with an accusing glare. "I fail to see the difference."

A ripple of outrage passed among the elves' group, and they extended their weapons once again.

"How dare you!" said one of the elves. "We are far superior to the fairies."

"In your dreams," Rosalyn said from behind me.

"Hang on!" I found myself wishing I stood anywhere except between the fairies and the elves, but if I moved, they might well start firing lightning bolts at one another. "Can you pick another time to fight? I need to escort Mrs Hansen from the forest before she gets into trouble."

"You would stand between us and justice?" said Bramble.

"Hey, don't shoot the messenger," I said. "Mrs Hansen,

we should go and ask the police how the search for Laurel is going."

"I don't have to listen to the likes of you," she spat. "As for the police, they've done a mediocre job of searching for Laurel. My daughter should be back home where she belongs."

"I don't disagree that the police have improvements to make, but you need to let them do their jobs and not make all our lives more difficult."

She advanced on me with a snarl, shoving one of the elves out of the way as she did so. The elf swung his tree branch, while she pulled out her wand in retaliation. The fairies closed in behind me, eager to get into the fray. If I didn't think of a solution fast, I'd get stuck in the middle of a three-way battle.

"Stop!" I pulled out my own wand, only for a blast of bright green light to skim past my shoulder and collide with Mrs Hansen.

At once, she froze in mid-motion, greenness slithering over her skin and solidifying until she turned the mottled colour of bark. Branches replaced her arms, and her head became lost in a cloud of leaves that formed the tree that was now all that remained of Mrs Hansen.

"Now you've done it," I said to nobody in particular, not entirely sure who'd cast the spell on her.

"I think it's an improvement," Rosalyn remarked.

"Agreed," said Ani. "Did you cast the spell?"

"No," said Rosalyn. "I thought it was you."

"Don't look at me." I turned in the direction I'd seen the flash come from and saw Conor lurking behind a nearby oak tree. "Be right back. Please don't attack each other while I'm gone."

I beat my wings and flew after Conor, waylaying him before he could slip away. "Conor, did you turn her into a tree?"

"I think I showed admirable restraint, all things considered," he said.

"You did, but you can't just leave her like that."

"I wasn't planning to," he said, "but if I undo the spell while those elves are still around, they might do worse than turn her into a tree."

"Fair point," I said. "Okay, we'll wait for everyone else to leave then change her back."

Rosalyn and Ani were already on their way towards me, seeing Conor. Giggling, they ran over. "Did *you* turn her into a tree?"

I turned back towards the elves and spotted one of them poking at Mrs Hansen's tree with a stick.

"Don't do that." I approached them, debating how to politely tell them to leave so we could turn her back into a human. "I haven't seen the Elf King for a while."

"So you haven't," Bramble growled. "I imagine he'll have words to say about *this*."

"That's right." I put on an encouraging tone. "We should go and see him. I'd like to have a chat with him."

Bramble shot the tree a glare. "We will take you to him."

I hadn't counted on an impromptu meeting with the elves' leader, but if it kept them away from Mrs Hansen while she was turned back into a person *and* stopped them from getting into a public fight with the fairies, I was more than happy to keep them distracted.

Time to see the Elf King.

6

I entered the elves' part of the forest, following Bramble and the others. Even now, I still easily got lost on the winding tracks among the ancient trees and the thickets of bright plants that I was fairly sure didn't exist in most non-magical woods.

As we walked, more elves popped up from the bushes, wielding sharpened branches. They seemed to be armed more heavily than usual, no doubt because of their unwelcome visitor. Their hostile expressions vanished when they recognised me, so I ignored the weapons and kept on walking.

The Elf King lived inside a giant hollow tree, and as we approached, its sprawling roots opened out to reveal a tunnel extending deep within. Even with my fairy guise on, I had to duck my head to get inside and crawl through in a highly undignified manner. I straightened upright inside the cave, where the Elf King sat on a tree stump decorated to resemble a throne. Gold leaves patterned his otherwise plain clothes.

"Blair Wilkes," he said. "It's been quite some time since we last saw one another."

"Ah, yeah, I've been busy."

In truth, I hadn't been quite sure what the elves would make of the fairies' arrival in town. They'd been among the first to predict their return, and they hadn't objected to Conor living in hiding in the woods for years... if they'd actually known he was there, that is. I wasn't too certain on that one.

"Yes," he said. "You've taken it upon yourself to help the fairies settle into town, have you not?"

"I'm doing my best to," I admitted, "but it's been a challenge. I don't know if you heard about the missing human girl, but she's been gone for a few days now, and she disappeared somewhere in the forest."

"That is no reason for her mother to trample through our part of the forest." He stiffened when Bramble approached and said something in an undertone. "So she believes *we* took our child?"

"She's blaming the fairies," I said. "But she was arguing with Bramble and the others earlier and throwing accusations around before one of the fairies turned her into a tree. Not that she didn't deserve it."

The Elf King eyed me. "If she comes onto our territory again, then she alone is responsible for whatever fate befalls her."

"I know, but she's trying to find her missing daughter," I said. "Are you sure you haven't seen or heard any signs of her?"

The Elf King spoke to Bramble again, who moved towards the back of the tunnel. Then he returned and set a shoe down on the floor.

A child's shoe.

"Is that—" I broke off. "It's not hers, is it?"

"A guard patrol found that in our territory," growled the Elf King. "I assume it belongs to a human."

My stomach lurched. So Laurel *had* been in this part of the forest. "She was here? When did you find it?"

"This morning."

So it's true. "She's still somewhere in here. But nobody has seen any signs of her?"

"If they have, they haven't said a word to me," he said.

I glanced around at the other elves. "But you found her shoe. She's been in this part of the forest. Why has nobody seen her at all?"

"That, I cannot say," said the Elf King. "You're asking the wrong person."

"Do *you* think someone took her?" I asked. "Because that's what her mother thinks. But she's letting her prejudices about fairies cloud her judgement."

A ripple of distaste spread among the other elves.

"They think we are the same as the fairies," Bramble said. "They are wrong."

"I know they're wrong," I said, having to raise my voice to be heard over the growing discontent among the elves. "Nobody in their right mind agrees with them."

"Except for a few foolish humans," added the Elf King.

The others stopped objecting when they heard their king speak, presumably not wanting to contradict his word.

"Exactly," I said. "If not for Laurel's disappearance, they wouldn't have bothered you. I'm sorry she came to your territory, though. I don't agree with her views on the fairies or on the elves. They deserve to be here as much as you do."

"The fairies have the right to live here in the forest," agreed the Elf King, "but they need to refrain from causing arguments with the humans. There are some who see us as the same and will blame my fellow elves, which I cannot allow."

"They won't cause any trouble." Unless one counted Conor turning Mrs Hansen into a tree, but the outcome might have been worse if he hadn't.

"Then I hope it does not happen again," he said. "Farewell, Blair Wilkes."

Dismissed. Two other elves flanked me as I crouched and crawled back through the tunnel again. I hadn't realised the humans' anti-fairy attitude would potentially cover the elves, too, but it made a kind of sense. The two were vaguely related, they had similar territorial tendencies, and the majority didn't seem inclined to mingle with humans. But that meant if one of the groups *had* taken Laurel captive, the rumours would spread to the other too. I wasn't convinced any of them had anything to do with her disappearance despite the shoe found on the elves' territory, but we needed to find the real kidnapper before the wrong person—or people—took the blame.

When I left the elves' territory, it was to find my dad waiting for me near the path that led to the fairies' homes.

"Hey, Dad," I said. "I was just seeing the elves. Do you come here often?"

"I've been to the elves' part of the forest a couple of times since my return to town," he said. "To visit the King."

"He offered you shelter while you were on the run, right?" I said. "Does that make you friends?"

"He did," said my dad. "Not all the elves are fond of my kind, but he did me a huge favour, for which I owe him a debt."

"Oh." I had the inkling he didn't mean the monetary kind of debt. Fairies and elves approached favours differently than humans did. "I wanted to get the elves away from the fairies before Conor turned Mrs Hansen human again. Is she still around?"

"Not at the moment," he said. "Why?"

I held up the shoe. "Some of the elves found this while they were patrolling. I think... I think it belongs to Laurel."

His expression shadowed. "That's not a good sign. I'll have to hand it over to Mrs Hansen if she's willing to listen to me without retaliating."

"Wait. The fairies did turn her from a tree back into a human again, didn't they?" I said.

"Yes, but she's even unhappier than before," he said. "After Conor undid the spell on her, I managed to convince her to leave the forest. Reluctantly."

That figured. "I guess telling her we found her daughter's shoe on the elves' territory wouldn't help matters."

"No," he said. "I think she'd take it as confirmation of her worst fears."

"Because she thinks the fairies and elves are the same," I said. "The Elf King told me."

"It's preposterous, but people like her aren't known for nuanced thinking," Dad said. "I hoped she might see the error of her ways, but with her daughter still missing for this long..."

"I know."

Where *was* she? You'd think she'd have run into one of the elves if she'd been so close to the centre of their territory, and if that was the case, they'd have informed their king at once.

Unless they hadn't.

Unless one of them had taken her.

But what proof did I have… and what reason would an elf possibly have to capture a human child?

———

Work passed quickly the following day, though my progress with the database remained as slow as ever. It didn't help that the previous day's events weighed on the back of my mind. Rob and I hadn't yet discussed our encounter near the university campus, but it had to be in his thoughts as well. As far as I was aware, Laurel's shoe had been returned to her mother via the police, but I wasn't sure if the werewolf knew the latest update on the search.

After leaving work, I waited for him outside the office. The blond werewolf was the last to leave, following his cousin, Callie, the receptionist.

"Hey, Blair," he said. "Something up?"

"Have the werewolves found any more signs of Laurel?" I asked.

"No," he said. "Did something else happen?"

"One of her shoes turned up on the elves' territory," I admitted. "They denied having anything to do with her disappearance, but I know there's a spot where your territory borders on theirs, and I wondered if anyone saw anything."

"Ah." He frowned. "So she was definitely in the woods, then."

"What would make you think otherwise?" I asked.

"Well, she's stayed alive for this long, so either she's been surviving on wild mushrooms or someone's been feeding her," he said. "Which means she's in someone's home."

Good point. It'd been days, and few kids were resourceful enough to survive that long in a semi-hostile magical forest without sustenance. When I'd been that age, my foster parents had hardly let me out of their sight. It was no wonder her mother was so hysterical. Yet the circumstances did seem to point to someone taking care of her, kidnappers or not.

"True," I allowed. "Okay, see you tomorrow."

I waved him off and headed to my magic lesson. Today would be a practical one, a nice change of pace from our theory lesson the other day, but not what I really needed on a day on which my focus levels were low. Especially when Rita announced we'd be learning to cast localised weather spells, which put me in mind of the magical lightning storms some fairies and elves could conjure up if the need arose. I'd yet to learn how to use that particular branch of my fairy magic, but I hadn't particularly enjoyed being on the receiving end either.

"To start off with," said Rita, "we'll learn the basic wand movements for making it rain. Copy me, both of you. We'll try with the sticks first before moving on to using your wands if I think you're ready."

In unison, Rebecca and I picked up the narrow sticks

we used to rehearse wand movements and did our best to mimic Rita as she moved her wand in a swishing motion. Rita corrected our positions with her usual forthrightness.

"Blair, aim higher and more to the left. There." She gave a nod as I followed her instructions. "Good. Now, pick up your wand and try casting the spell for real. Like this."

Rita waved her wand, conjuring up a small cloud, which scattered several raindrops on the desk before she made it vanish.

I switched the stick for my wand and repeated the movements. A surge of glittery water shot from the end like a hosepipe, bouncing off the ceiling and splattering across the room.

"Ah!" I jumped to my feet, readying myself to clean up the mess. "Sorry."

"No worries." Rebecca picked up her own wand and executed a perfect banishment charm to clear away the glittery water without seeming fazed in the slightest. She'd come a long way in recent weeks.

I, on the other hand, appeared to be heading backwards. Poor Rebecca didn't fare much better, though she at least made water appear without any glitter.

"At least one of you is making an effort," Rita said.

I wilted on the spot. "Sorry. I'll try harder next time."

On my fifteenth attempt, I finally managed to conjure up a rain cloud, but instead of hovering on the spot, it went sweeping around the room and drenched Rita's desk before she made it vanish. When our lesson came to an end, it didn't surprise me when Rita beckoned me to stay behind.

After Rebecca had closed the door behind her, I readied myself for another repudiation. "Sorry."

"I know, Blair," said Rebecca. "Madame Grey wants to see you."

My nerves spiked. "She does?"

She hadn't come near the classroom, that I'd seen, so it couldn't be about my lack of progress in my magic lessons. *I hope.*

"Yes," she said. "You don't want to keep her waiting, do you?"

"No, of course not. See you at our next lesson." I fled the room and halted outside Madame Grey's office, taking in a deep breath while knocking on the door.

"Come in." Madame Grey beckoned me inside her neat office from where she sat in front of several neatly arranged bookshelves. "Blair."

I walked into the room, wariness settling over me. She hadn't witnessed my disaster of a magic lesson, but she didn't need to watch my every move to know that Laurel's disappearance and the fairies were at the forefront of my mind.

"Rita said you wanted to talk to me," I said.

She looked up from her paperwork on her desk. "Yes. I see we already have a dozen new fairy residents in town, and more applications are coming through every day."

"They're sending them straight to you?" I asked.

"Your father is, yes," she said. "Why do you ask?"

"Just curious." Not all the newcomers in town had visited the coven before they moved here in person, though there was also Oak to think of, who'd spurned the witches altogether. I couldn't think of a long-term way to deal with him that wouldn't involve another angry outburst on his part, but he had to accept eventually that the quickest route to being accepted was to get it over with. Until then, I'd keep my distance from him.

Madame Grey studied my face, giving the unnerving impression she knew I was hiding something from her. "You've been spending a lot of time in the forest lately, haven't you?"

"I know Laurel is still missing," I said carefully. "Did you hear the elves found her shoe on their territory yesterday?"

"Yes, I did," she said. "I also heard you intervened in a conflict between the elves and the fairies yourself."

"I didn't know what else to do," I said. "Mrs Hansen was provoking both of them until Conor turned her into a tree."

She wrinkled her nose. "No doubt that was the best outcome for her, all things considered."

"Yeah." I shifted from one foot to the other. "I thought it might distract the elves if I went to visit their king, but I didn't expect them to have found Laurel's shoe."

"An unfortunate development," said Madame Grey, "but I don't think that necessarily implicates anyone in particular in her disappearance. You've been to the university campus a couple of times, too, haven't you?"

"Yes, I went to the library." Why did she care? I'd thought Madame Grey was happy to let me do as I liked, even where the fairies were concerned.

"From what I hear," she said, "the staff have since received several complaints about missing posters depicting... fairies."

Ah. "They were awful posters. Someone drew these horrible caricatures of fairies kidnapping human children, and a couple of the other fairies saw the posters and were rightly furious. I didn't know how else to handle it. Removing them the regular way would have taken too long. Besides, Samuel implied it was fine to take them down."

"I see." The disapproving note in her voice made my heart sink, even though I had no regrets about shredding those posters to ribbons. "Blair, it's best for you not to provoke that particular group of students. I would prefer for the poor girl to be found with as minimal an impact as possible—both on the fairies and on everyone else."

"You think Rodney and his friends will think the fairies removed their posters?" I couldn't keep the scepticism out of my voice. "They were the ones who disturbed the fairies in their homes to begin with, so they deserved it, anyway."

"I don't condone their actions," said Madame Grey. "I only question the necessity of your involvement."

"I want the fairies to feel as welcome here as I did," I said. "That's all."

"Of course, Blair," she said. "Just remember we're all under scrutiny at the moment, and so are you. You may leave."

"Okay." I walked out of her office before my mouth got me into even more trouble. On the whole, I'd almost have preferred a lecture on my ineptitude at magic lessons. I refused to regret removing those posters, but I wished I'd been able to do something more to quell the rumours that had led to their creation in the first place.

Like finding Laurel Hansen, for instance.

Given how recently her shoe had been found, she couldn't have gone far, and her mother might well have found her if she and Rodney's friends hadn't spent so much time pestering the fairies instead. Nathan, of course, was doing his best to make up for the police's shortfalls and had been sending out patrols frequently to make sure they covered every inch of the forest and the border in search of Laurel.

The odds of her having left the town itself were low. If someone had taken her, they must be within the forest itself… which led me straight back to the elves.

At home, I found Alissa in the living room with Nina, our upstairs flatmate. Nina, who worked as a hairdresser, had been giving Alissa a haircut, judging by the pile of dark curls on the carpet.

"Hey, Nina." I ditched my coat and shoes before finding Sky napping on the sofa and sitting next to him.

"Hey, Blair." Nina banished the discarded hair with a wave of her wand. "How's it going? You were at a magic lesson, right?"

"Yeah, with Rebecca." When Sky woke up, I gave him a stroke, and he purred sleepily. "How're you doing?"

"Not too bad." Nina glanced at Alissa, who was making tea in the kitchen. "I heard about that missing girl…"

I suppressed a groan. "I suppose the gossip has got around the whole town by now."

"I don't think the fairies did it," she said. "Just for the record. I was just telling Alissa that I've talked to my customers about it this week, and they don't seem to think the fairies did it either. They think the girl got lost in the woods."

"Yeah." I petted Sky, who purred again, his eyes half closed. "Her mother's irrationally obsessed with the fairies, and I think it started before her kid disappeared, to tell you the truth."

"Looked that way." Alissa carried three teacups over to the table and distributed them among the three of us. "Don't pay her any attention, Blair. Did your magic lesson go well?"

I pulled a face. "Not really. I've a lot on my mind."

"Samuel said you were at the university campus yesterday," said Alissa. "You never mentioned you saw one another."

I picked up my tea and blew on it to cool it. "I got distracted by everything that happened afterwards."

I'd given her a rundown of my misadventures yesterday, from my encounter with the fairies on campus to Mrs Hansen's brief stint as a tree and my subsequent visit to the Elf King. I hadn't really gone into much depth about the part involving the posters or Samuel's implied permission to sneakily remove them.

"Yes, I gathered," she said. "He said you complained about some posters and wanted to take them down."

"Did he mention they showed caricatures of fairies capturing human children?" I asked. "They were put up by those students who were pestering the fairies with Mrs Hansen the other day. A couple of the fairies found out and got mad, so I helped them take down the posters without anyone noticing."

"Except the people who put them there," said Alissa. "Who complained to the coven leaders."

That would explain how Madame Grey had found out. "They do know those same students were harassing members of the public, don't they? Your grandmother was pretty dismissive when I tried to tell her."

"I don't disagree, Blair," she said. "You were right to remove them, but... well. My grandmother told me Mrs Hansen is raising a fuss with anyone in the area who might listen to her. She even called the local branch of the hunters to ask them to get involved."

"Seriously?" My throat went dry. "Madame Grey didn't tell me that."

No wonder she'd been so short with me earlier. While the hunters' leader was no longer a threat to any of us, that didn't mean his views weren't shared by others in town.

"Wow." Nina drained her teacup. "I thought the hunters were pretty much obsolete, though. They still don't have a new leader, do they?"

"I don't know if anyone's taken the Inquisitor's place yet," I said, "but they do have local branch leaders who are still in place. It wouldn't surprise me if they wanted to avoid our town for the foreseeable future, though."

"Good," said Alissa. "Mrs Hansen wasn't able to get hold of anyone who'd listen to her, for the record. Just the fact that she tried was enough to alarm my grandmother."

"She's trouble, all right." Nina rose to her feet. "Blair, want a haircut before I go home?"

"Nah, I have a date in less than an hour," I said. "Another day?"

"Sure," she said. "Have fun."

As she departed our flat, I slumped back on the sofa. "Mrs Hansen just won't quit, will she?"

"She wants her daughter back," said Alissa. "I can't believe she's been gone this long."

"Yeah... but the elves found her shoe yesterday," I said.

"That proves she's alive. Maybe she's hiding from her mother. Can't say I'd blame her for that."

Alissa made a noncommittal noise. "Maybe."

"You don't think they kidnapped her?" I said. "The fairies? Or the elves?"

"I don't," she said, "but they do strange things sometimes, don't they? And some of the stories my grandmother told me… well. The rumours started for a reason."

"They're just stories," I said, a little stung that Alissa, of all people, was taking them seriously.

"I know they are, but even the normal world has the same kind of stories as we do," said Alissa. "Right?"

"Yeah." I rubbed my tired eyes. "Doesn't make them accurate."

All the same, other stories about the paranormal had turned out to hold a kernel of truth within them. What if the same was true of the fairies?

7

I hoped my date with Nathan that evening might take my mind off my lingering worries about Laurel's disappearance and the ongoing shame of my earlier encounter with Madame Grey. Not to mention the rumours of fairies kidnapping human children lurking at the back of my mind. And it did, for a bit. Nathan picked me up from my house, and we walked to the pub, chatting about inconsequential things.

No sooner had we reached the Troll's Tavern, however, than Nathan checked his phone and stopped before entering the pub. "Steve wants me to come to the police station."

"Why?" Couldn't the gargoyle leave us alone for a single evening?

"Probably an update on Laurel's disappearance," he said grimly. "You don't have to come."

"I want to," I told him. "If Mrs Hansen is involved, I need to warn my dad in case she starts bothering the other fairies again."

What might have happened this time? Worry swirled inside me as we headed to the police station. One of the town's newer constructions, it towered over its neighbours with its hulking grey walls exuding menace. I didn't see any fairies or elves through the clear glass front doors, but Mrs Hansen stood next to the unimpressed-looking receptionist, Claire, and a tall, lean man I didn't know. Not a fairy. My paranormal senses pinpointed him as human but stopped there. He couldn't be a normal, could he?

"Who's that?" I whispered to Nathan.

"No idea." He took the lead through the automatic doors into the police station, where we found Erin and Buck standing against the opposite wall, out of range of Mrs Hansen's ranting. Sensible idea, really.

"What's going on?" Nathan asked them in an undertone.

"Mrs Hansen's ex-husband showed up," Buck muttered in reply. "Laurel's father, Pierce Reynold."

"Oh." I hadn't known Mrs Hansen was divorced, but it explained why nobody had kicked up a fuss about her covering her house in fairy-proof flowers and wandering around the forest getting into trouble. Pierce Reynold's arrival might complicate the situation, though, especially if he was as anti-fairy as his ex-wife.

"Yeah, let's just say it wasn't an amicable split," Erin said in an undertone. "Sure you want to be here, Blair?"

Mrs Hansen raised her voice from across the room. "I won't hear another word of this. You dare to show up here, *days* after your daughter disappears, without a word of apology?"

I didn't hear her ex-husband's reply, but Mrs Hansen scoffed in return.

"It wouldn't surprise me if you were the one who spirited her away yourself," she said. "It's what you wanted, isn't it? You waited until my back was turned and then stole her away."

I goggled at her then at the tall pale man looking calmly at his ex. Definitely not a fairy, but there was something odd about him all the same. Why wasn't my paranormal-sensing power reacting to him?

"You're the one who was careless enough to lose her," said Pierce. "You have some nerve blaming me for your inadequate parenting skills. You left her unwatched in the garden when the forest is right there, didn't you?"

"How dare you blame me!" she shrieked. "This town used to be safe enough for a child to walk around alone, inside and outside of the forest, but now these outsiders have shown up, none of our children will be safe. Laurel was the first they took, but she won't be the last, mark my words."

"Enough," said Claire, the receptionist. "Take your argument outside, please."

The two of them ignored her and continued their glare-off with one another. Claire, meanwhile, went to the back office and rapped on the door, presumably looking for backup.

"I'm not leaving," said Pierce. "I want my daughter back. Why did you leave her alone in the garden to begin with?"

Mrs Hansen's face flushed. "I went into the house for five minutes. When I returned, she was gone. Someone took her."

Lie.

I froze, trying to keep my expression blank. I hadn't been thinking about my lie-sensing power, because the sudden appearance of a new suspect had taken me off guard. Question was, what was she lying about? And was her ex lying too? His appearance seemed a tad late, considering his daughter had been missing for days.

"Someone took her, and you decided not to tell me until several days after the fact?" said Pierce. "Don't blame me for not being around when you didn't *tell* me she was missing."

"I didn't expect you to show your face here," she said. "After all, you've missed almost every milestone in her life. Why should this be any different?"

"Ooh," Erin murmured. "Things are heating up. I'm Team Pierce, for the record."

Buck shook his head at her, but he didn't say anything to contradict her word.

I shuffled closer to Nathan and said in a low voice, "Does this mean she's going to stop blaming the fairies?"

"I wouldn't count on it," he said out of the corner of his mouth.

If Mrs Hansen's ex turned out to be to blame, at least it'd take some of the attention off the fairies, but Laurel's shoe had turned up in the forest, and the odds of someone from outside the town planting it there were pretty low.

Still... I couldn't help wondering how many more lies they'd both told. The two of them stood nose to nose, glaring at one another, completely oblivious to the rest of us watching the show.

"Every word you say is a lie," Mrs Hansen said. "Why should I trust you?"

"Why should I trust *you?*" Pierce retaliated. "You're the one who *lost our child!*"

"I did not!"

My lie-sensing power chose that moment to react, but it was beyond me to tell who it pointed to. Maybe both of them were being untruthful. Their shouting had begun to give me a headache, but if I left the police station, Nathan and Erin would be stuck here with them until Steve deigned to show his face. I assumed he was hiding somewhere in the back to avoid the bickering exes, but someone had to act before this got even more out of hand.

I cleared my throat. "If it helps, my magical talent allows me to sense truth from lie. I can clear up who's telling the truth if you like."

Mrs Hansen wheeled on me. "You can tell truth from lie, can you? A likely story."

"It's my witch talent." It was technically a result of the weird combination of my fairy and witch magic, but I didn't want to further provoke her ire by mentioning the fairies again. "I can tell whether anything anyone says is a lie or the truth."

"Will you let Blair ask you a couple of questions?" Nathan stepped in, addressing both Pierce and his furious ex-wife. "It seems a more efficient way to resolve this dilemma than by shouting unfounded accusations."

"We most certainly will not," Mrs Hansen said. "This is our business. Not yours."

"You're the one broadcasting our business for the world to hear," said her ex-husband. "If this witch can read truth from lie, I'd say it's worth using her talent to find out what you're hiding from me."

"I'm not hiding any—"

"Oh, let her do it," Erin interjected. "Come on, both of you. You know it's much easier than tossing blame around without any proof. Blair, ask both of them if they're lying."

"Um, it has to be more specific than that." Flustered by all the eyes on me, I scrambled for an explanation. "I have to ask a precise question. Or someone else can ask the questions if you'd prefer."

Mrs Hansen scowled. "Can you tell if *anyone* is lying?"

"Almost everyone." Not ghosts, but I didn't think that was what she was implying. "It'll work on everyone in this room, anyway."

There was only one living person my ability hadn't worked on: the Inquisitor, the strongest fairy I'd ever met. Not only had I been unable to tell whether a word he'd said had been truth or lie, but I'd also been completely unable to see through the glamour he used to hide his fairy appearance, and I'd had to deploy the power of the Seeing Stone in order to expose him. For all I knew, some of the other fairies had a similar level of talent. Oak, for one, had an unusually strong skill at glamour, based on the elaborate trap he'd thrown Buck into. Pierce, though, registered as plain old human, which instantly raised my suspicions. What if he was hiding something too?

"Fine," Pierce said. "We'll do it."

He can't be hiding anything if he'll willingly subject himself to my lie-sensing power, right?

A hush fell over the reception area, and my face heated as several pairs of eyes fixed on me. "Okay. Both of you, can you tell me when you last saw Laurel?"

"I haven't seen Laurel since the last time she and her mother came to visit," Pierce said.

True.

My gaze slid to Mrs Hansen, whose scowl deepened. "I last saw her in the garden shortly before she disappeared, but we both know this questioning is pointless. Pierce, did you take Laurel away with you?"

"No, I did not."

True. "He's telling the truth. No lies."

"There you have it," said Pierce. "I didn't take her."

"Stop being so smug!" said Mrs Hansen. "Laurel is still missing. If you didn't take her, then it must have been those fairies. Exactly as I suspected."

Here we go again. "We already searched the fairies' part of the forest," I said. "They didn't take her. I'd have known if they'd been lying too."

Pierce frowned. "There really are fairies living in the forest now?"

"Yes." Defensiveness leaked into my tone. "Your ex-wife seems to be under the impression that every single fairy is hell-bent on kidnapping human children. I'm not entirely sure if this obsession started before or after Laurel's disappearance, but there's zero proof."

"How dare you mock me!" Mrs Hansen spluttered. "Laurel disappeared in a forest teeming with monsters, and she's still out there. Of course one of them is keeping her captive."

Pierce turned on me. "Have you questioned *all* the suspects using that lie-sensing power of yours?"

"I don't work for the police," I said. "Also, I thought your ex-wife didn't want me involved."

"Why didn't you want her help?" Pierce addressed Mrs Hansen again.

"Because *she's* one of those fairies." Mrs Hansen spat out the words. "They're the ones who took her. I know it."

Pierce's eyes rounded with understanding. "You're a fairy? Really?"

"I'm half fairy," I clarified. "And the fairies didn't take your daughter. Most of them just moved to town, and all they want is to be left alone."

His expression cleared. "That explains her... ah, fixation on the fairies if they're new to town."

"There are two of them in this very room," Erin said with a glance at Buck. "I'd watch what you say."

"See?" Mrs Hansen exploded. "They're masquerading as humans. That proves they're liars, does it not?"

"It's called glamour," I explained when Pierce's gaze turned back to me. "If they want, fairies can put on the guise of a human in order to blend in. The fairies in the forest, though, they don't use it, for the most part. They don't need to."

Nathan cleared his throat. "To return to the subject at hand, we've been doing all we can to find your daughter, but it's unlikely anyone living in the fairies' part of the woods took her. If they had, we would have tracked her down."

"Her shoe was found on the fairies' territory," said Mrs Hansen insistently. "If you bothered showing your face here, Pierce, you'd have known."

My heart sank when Pierce's mouth thinned into a line. "You found her shoe on the fairies' territory?"

"No, it was near the elves' part of the forest," I said. "Not the fairies. They aren't the same." *No matter what your ex seems to think,* I silently added, managing to refrain from saying that part aloud.

"I see." A pregnant pause followed his words as if he was reconsidering assigning blame after all. Of course, it was easier for both of them to blame a faceless group of people than admit they'd failed to keep a close enough watch on their daughter, but that didn't make it okay.

"We have no proof she was taken," Nathan said. "Laurel's shoe was found in the forest, without any other signs of her or anyone else nearby."

Except for the elves who'd found it, but they wouldn't have had any reason to hide the truth from me, would they?

Mrs Hansen sucked in a breath. "I think you're covering for them. Both of you. I expected better from our town's security team."

"We've searched the forest extensively," Nathan told Pierce. "And, of course, we've questioned everyone and found no proof that anyone has a motive for taking her."

Mrs Hansen jabbed a finger at me. "*She* hasn't questioned them."

"I told you I don't work for the police." *She can't be serious.* I'd been the first to welcome most of the new fairies to town. Turning interrogator would erase all the goodwill between us and would make them look as suspiciously on me as they did at the people trying to make them feel unwelcome.

On the other hand, if there was the slightest chance someone among the fairies might not be a hundred percent trustworthy—someone like Oak, who reacted with hostility when I'd simply wanted to help him introduce himself to Madame Grey—then perhaps I ought to push past my discomfort and speak to him again. If he didn't turn me into a tree or knock me into a hole in the ground, anyway. No, interrogating Oak was off the table until he'd got over his distrust of the witches, which might never happen given their unpleasant history.

I didn't want to explain *that* to Mrs Hansen—or her ex, for that matter. The other fairies, though… if Mrs Hansen actually believed my lie-sensing abilities were accurate enough to clear up the matter, perhaps the quickest way to get her to leave them alone would be to ask a couple of simple questions with her as a witness and then let it go.

My thoughts must have shown on my face, because Nathan edged closer to me.

"You don't have to if you don't want to, Blair," he said in a low voice.

"I know," I whispered back. Raising my voice, I addressed Mrs Hansen. "If I ask the fairies a couple of questions and it turns out they don't know anything about your missing daughter, will you please agree to leave them alone afterwards?"

"Yes," said Pierce, though I hadn't been asking him. "I'd say that's more than fair, right, Abigail?"

"I suppose," said Mrs Hansen, as if she hadn't been calling me a liar not ten minutes beforehand. "Let's go."

"Ah… it's probably better if you stay behind," I said hastily. "They might think they're being threatened if I bring you with me."

"Why, how dare you," she said. "Why would they make that assumption?"

"Because you were literally threatening them the other day."

Pierce stifled a laugh then cut it off with a cough. "Stay here, Abigail, and tell me all about your encounter with the fairies while Blair speaks to them."

Mrs Hansen raised her voice to launch into another

argument with him, at which point I slipped out of the police station with Nathan and left them to it. A moment later, Erin and Buck followed us.

"I'm only coming with you to get away from those two," Erin said. "I won't get in the way of your questioning."

"Same," Buck added. "I can see why the pair of them split up. She's a nightmare."

"Is Steve hiding from her?" I asked. "Or is he still in the forest?"

"Hiding in the back room, I bet," Erin said. "What're you going to do, pretend to question them and then tell her they're all innocent? That's what I'd do."

"I don't know," I admitted. "I want to clear up the whole thing, but how can I question the fairies without making them feel like I'm trying to interrogate them? I guess they don't know about my lie-sensing talent, but it's not like I've got a good reason to start hassling them again."

"I'll help," Nathan offered. "We'll handle it, Blair."

I gave him a smile, taking his hand as we headed towards the forest. It wasn't much of a double date—and thanks to our interrupted meal, I was starving—but I doubted Mrs Hansen would much appreciate it if we sneaked off to the Troll's Tavern instead. The idea was tempting, but so was the notion of getting Mrs Hansen off my back and convincing her to leave the fairies alone in one fell swoop.

At the edge of the forest, however, several were gargoyles gathered in the road near the house Mrs Hansen had decorated in fairy-proof flowers. We came to an abrupt halt, my heart sinking when I saw Steve among their group. He hadn't been hiding in the office at the police station after all.

Nathan approached him. "Is something else going on?"

"What are you doing here?" The nearest gargoyle eyed me. "Come to barge into our investigation again, have you?"

"No, I'm here to speak to the fairies," I said. "Are you looking for Mrs Hansen? Because she's at the police station with her ex-husband right now, and I think Claire would appreciate it if you came to help calm them down."

"Mrs Hansen will have to wait," said the gargoyle. "Another child has disappeared."

8

Oh, no.

"Who disappeared?" asked Nathan. "Where?"

"Rhiannon Bradley," said one of the gargoyles. "She lives with her parents, two doors down from Laurel Hansen's house. Their garden backs onto the forest."

My heart sank. "So it's the same as Laurel, then."

"Sounds that way," Erin murmured, her mouth turning down at the corners. "Might she have been looking for Laurel?"

The gargoyle glanced over his shoulder to where Steve stood talking to a distraught-looking witch and wizard outside one of the houses bordering the forest. "Steve's talking to the girl's family, so if you don't want to draw his attention, Blair, I'd strongly suggest you leave."

"I was going to talk to the fairies anyway, but I'd be happy to help with the search." Steve would be less than thrilled at my involvement, but I hardly cared less what he thought. *Another child vanished.* The instant Mrs Hansen

88

found out, she'd have twice the reason to hurl the blame at the fairies. "We can cover more ground between us."

"Are you sure?" asked Nathan.

"I'm sure."

Steve might kick up a fuss if I did question the fairies, but it wasn't as though any of the gargoyles had lie-sensing powers. With two children missing, it'd become even more urgent that I cleared up the matter of the fairies' potential involvement as quickly as possible. I was certain the fairies hadn't taken Rhiannon either, but if Mrs Hansen found out, she'd be ready to storm into the forest and raise hell.

Nathan and I entered the forest, where the canopy of branches cut off most of the remaining sunlight. It was already evening, so we wouldn't have long to search before it got too dark to see where we were going. Nathan, Erin, and Buck spread out to search the surrounding area without going too far from the path, while I approached the brightening path that led into the fairies' territory.

The strange between-world that the fairies occupied already seemed bigger than the last time I'd been here. They were spreading out, putting down roots, and the idea of any of them being forced to leave broke my heart to contemplate. As I walked into the clearing, I spotted Conor roaming around outside the cottages, perhaps having seen the gargoyles' approach from the forest. I caught his gaze and waved, but he didn't return the gesture. Curtains flickered in the windows of the nearby houses, indicating the fairies already expected an intrusion to come.

"Hey," I said to Conor. "Everything okay in here?"

"I heard another child vanished," he said. "Braden told me. He's searching the woods. If you want to help him, feel free."

"Have you spoken to the police yet?" I asked.

"I have not." His voice tightened around the edges. "If they intend to disturb my neighbours, I cannot say they would be welcome."

My throat closed up. "I know it's not ideal, but Mrs Hansen is still hassling the police, and it wouldn't surprise me if she used the second child's disappearance as an excuse to keep pressuring them to come back. Maybe it's better if I talk to them instead. The residents, I mean, not the police."

I knew I was babbling, but Conor was sometimes unpredictable, and he'd drenched me with a magically conjured thunderstorm in a temper before. This time, however, all he did was narrow his eyes. "You want to interrogate the other fairies?"

"I wouldn't put it that way," I said. "Come on, do you really want Steve coming back here and pestering every-one? If I confirm none of them was involved, he'll leave you alone, and so will the other gargoyles."

"If he believes you," said Conor. "I confess myself sceptical."

With good reason. Given Steve's attempted intrusion into his house the other day, I didn't blame the fairy for being reluctant to believe he'd leave us alone. What Conor *didn't* know about was my lie-sensing power, because I'd wanted to minimise the potential conflict that might result from mentioning my mother's side of the family in front of the fairies, since her ancestors' actions were still a sore spot with some of them. Besides, it had never come up in conversation between us.

Unlike witches, fairies had largely the same kinds of magical talents at their disposal with little deviation—namely, the ability to use glamour and exert some control over the elements—and it simply wouldn't have occurred to any of them that my half-witch-half-fairy heritage might have resulted in a combination of both. Even my dad had admitted he hadn't realised at first how odd my talents might be.

Now was definitely not the time to mention my witch side, though, so I made a mental note to bring it up later when everyone had calmed down.

"Nathan will believe me, and he has influence with Steve," I said instead. "Erin and Buck do too. It's that or deal with gargoyles trampling through your flowerbeds all night."

Conor was silent for a moment. "If you're certain the gargoyles will leave us alone once you give them your word that none of the fairies have committed any crimes, then you're free to ask all the questions you like."

"I'm sure." I couldn't say the same for Mrs Hansen, of course, and I hoped the other missing girl's parents would be less likely to blame the fairies than she was. Though for all we knew, their disappearances weren't connected, and the second missing kid would show up during our search of the woods. Maybe they both would. One never knew.

I caught Rosalyn's eye from the other side of her window as I walked up to her door first. When I knocked, she answered right away. "Another kid disappeared in the forest, right?"

"Yeah, a human girl," I said. "Same place as last time. Have you seen any signs of her? Any human children?"

"No," she said. "I haven't seen any humans. Not until you showed up with your friends, anyway. Are they coming to question everyone?"

My lie-sensing power told me she spoke true, so I said, "Thanks for letting me know. I offered to question everyone instead of the police, so I'm hoping I can convince them to leave you alone."

"They suspect us, don't they?" she asked.

I shook my head. "No, the police don't. But Mrs Hansen is still hanging around, spewing her bile, and I thought it was better to clear this up before she can get involved even further."

Out of the corner of my eye, I spotted Conor passing by with an unreadable look on his face, which made me feel inexplicably guilty for using my lie-sensing powers. Did he suspect I might have other motives for being the one to do the questioning aside from the need to keep the gargoyles away? He said nothing, so I turned away from Rosalyn's house and went to the next one, trying to reassure myself that it wasn't as if I'd outright taken Steve's guilty-until-proven-innocent stance. I'd like to think I was a bit nicer with my questioning than the gargoyles were, but the fact remained that I was disturbing people who'd probably done nothing wrong. It didn't sit right with me.

To get it over with, I knocked on Ani's door next and repeated my questions. She answered promptly in the negative, and I moved to the next house. Conor continued to roam around in the background, while Nathan and the others waited farther back, no doubt keeping their eyes peeled for any signs of the gargoyles or Mrs Hansen.

To no surprise whatsoever, the other fairies exhibited no signs of having any idea where either of the missing girls had vanished to. After I'd spoken to them all, I rejoined Nathan, Erin, and Buck, and we made our way back to the regular part of the forest. Darkness had begun to sweep across the trees, which cast long shadows across the leaf-strewn paths.

"No problems?" asked Nathan.

"No lies either, but I didn't expect any of the fairies to be involved," I said. "I just had to appease Mrs Hansen. And the gargoyles. Has Steve come into the forest yet?"

"No," said Erin. "He claims midges keep biting him every time he comes into the forest, and he hates not being able to fly properly with the trees in the way."

I stifled a grin, wondering if the midges were due to one of Rosalyn's pranks. At least I'd established the fairies' innocence for my own peace of mind, but Oak remained on the suspect list, and I had yet to ask some pointed questions of the elves too. Not that the Elf King would appreciate it if I rampaged into his territory uninvited.

"Given Steve's temperament, I doubt he'll take your word for it," Buck added.

"He might," said Nathan. "I can try to work my powers of persuasion on him after we've finished our search."

"I heard my dad's searching the forest too," I recalled. "Should we go and find him? We don't have much time before it gets dark."

"Lead the way," said Erin. "I've got lost five times already, and I haven't even left this part of the forest yet."

"Believe me, I can relate."

Dad wouldn't have gone far from the fairies' home, so I led the way along the route that ended at the lake. The missing girl surely wouldn't have wandered this far away without being stumbled upon, but on the other hand, if her kidnappers had been witches or wizards, they might have used magic to take her anywhere. To find out if any traces of magic were at the scene where she'd disappeared, I'd need to ask Steve or the girl's parents, so I put the thought out of my mind for now, trying to shake away the image of a fairy descending and lifting the girl out of the garden…

Rustling in the bushes ahead made me grab my wand, and relief swept over me when I recognised my dad searching the nearby undergrowth.

"Hey," I called to him. "It's me."

"Blair?" he said. "You shouldn't be out here."

"I'm not alone." I indicated Nathan and the others behind me, who'd spread out to search the surrounding area. "I figured you could use some help. I already talked to all the fairies, in the hopes that it'd convince the police to leave them alone."

"You did?" he said. "Wait… you used your powers?"

Guilt flushed my cheeks, though there was no judgement in his tone. "I didn't want to break trust with them, but I figured it was better than them having to defend themselves to Steve with Mrs Hansen yelling in the background."

"She's not here in the forest, is she?" he said.

"No, but she's at the police station now," I said. "Her ex-husband showed up too. It was actually starting to look like she was going to blame him instead of the fairies, but then we came to the forest and found out the second girl was missing as well."

"It's terrible timing," my dad said. "I've been looking for an hour, and I've found no sign of either of the children."

"Me neither," I said. "I wonder if more of the fairies might want to get involved in helping with the search, though. They can see through illusions better than most people."

"Not all of them are as skilled as you are, Blair," he said.

My face flushed from his praise, I walked on, resuming my search of the forest. Minutes passed in relative silence, but my illusion-sensing powers didn't alert me to anything—until a flash of movement stirred out of the corner of my eye, and I nearly jumped out of my skin when Oak appeared from nowhere. Literally.

"Ah!" I pressed a hand to my chest, my heart slamming against my ribcage. "You're out of your house."

What in the world was he doing wandering around the forest at night? Aside from scaring me half to death, that is. The fairy walked barefoot, wearing a long robe-like garment that made him look like he'd been sleepwalking, but his eerily bright green eyes were wide awake.

"Well observed, human," he said. "I assume I am allowed to seek a change of scenery, according to the laws your coven values so highly?"

The laws didn't seem to matter to him when it came to actually telling the coven he lived here, but I managed to refrain from saying that aloud. "Did you hear about the other girl who went missing near the forest?"

His expression turned blank. "Who is she?"

"Her name's Rhiannon Bradley," I said. "She lives in the same street as the other girl who disappeared over the weekend, and she went missing in the woods this evening."

"How very careless of the humans to let her out of their sight."

"I wouldn't say that. The police think someone kidnapped both of the children, actually, and their parents are really worried." Annoyance over his casual tone pushed me to abandon caution and unleash my lie-sensing power on him. "Have you seen any humans in here?"

"I have seen far too many of your kind around."

"That's not what I meant." Did he know what I was doing? He couldn't know my lie-sensing powers existed, so maybe he was just being difficult on purpose. "I'm not all human, besides. Neither is Buck. Otherwise we wouldn't have been able to get out of your trap."

Dad walked up behind me. "Is there a problem, Oak?"

Oak swivelled to give him a withering look. "Nothing that concerns you, pretender."

And without another word, he turned heel and vanished, blending into the surrounding forest.

I turned back to my dad. "Is it usual for him to be wandering around here? I thought he never left his territory."

"It doesn't surprise me that he's become bold enough to go and explore," said Dad. "Not that I think it's advisable for him to walk out in public, but he'll take no direction from me."

"Does he *want* the coven to haul him in for questioning?" I shook my head. "The police don't know he's here, so he won't be on their suspect lists, but I told Mrs Hansen I'd question all the fairies to get her off my back. He counts too."

Of all the fairies living in the woods, Oak was by far the most likely suspect. His attitude towards humans in general was disdainful at best, he'd evaded my questions, and here he was, wandering around in the open right after a second kidnapping had occurred not far from here.

Whatever the case, two similar disappearances were unlikely to be a simple coincidence, and the odds were high that the same person or people had taken both of them. Oak's suspicious behaviour rang alarm bells in my mind, but I couldn't discount the possibility that my previous bad experiences with fairies were influencing my outlook on him. I'd fallen victim to the fairies' trickery on numerous occasions, and while my reunion with my dad had helped me see them in a different light, I hadn't entirely forgotten that some of the fairies had supported the hunters.

Was I right to be suspicious of Oak? It wasn't as if my thoughts were based in mindless prejudice like Mrs Hansen's attitude, but if he kept taking excursions, his presence would be exposed to the rest of the town sooner or later. Yet it seemed he wasn't in the least bit bothered by that possibility, and I had even less clue how to deal with *that*.

The paths darkened more and more as I walked until I tripped over a tree root and fell flat on my face.

"Blair, are you okay?" Nathan walked over to me and reached out a hand.

"Sure." I took his hand and let him pull me to my feet. "Wasn't looking where I was going."

"I think that's enough searching," he said. "It's too dark. Shifters have better eyesight to see at night."

"Guess fairies don't." I rubbed my forehead. "I hoped we'd find at least a trace of Rhiannon."

"Me too," he said. "I'm sorry, Blair, but I think we're going to have to go back."

"I need to tell Steve that I already questioned the fairies too," I said. "I hope he believes me and doesn't decide he needs to send a bunch of the other gargoyles to interrogate them as well."

"Yes… I hope so, too," said Nathan. "I'll do my best to convince him."

We tracked down Erin and Buck, and our group left the forest, trying not to feel like we were giving up. It wasn't as if there weren't any other places Rhiannon might have hidden outside of the forest, after all, and we still didn't know all the details of her own situation. Even with Laurel's mum, we hadn't known she had an ex-husband who might have been involved with her disappearance until today.

My heart sank when I heard Mrs Hansen's shrill tones emanating from the police station, as though she hadn't budged an inch since we'd left her to go to the forest. One look through the doors showed me her ex was still there, too, while another couple who must be Rhiannon's parents stood near the back of the reception area, talking to a pair of gargoyles.

Steve, meanwhile, accosted us at the door. "What are you doing here, Blair Wilkes?"

"I spoke to the fairies," I told him. "I used my lie-sensing powers to question every one of the fairies in the forest, and none of them took Laurel or Rhiannon."

"And I'm supposed to take your word for it?"

"Yes," Nathan said. "Blair's abilities are faultless. You know that."

"The fairies are tricksters," said Steve.

My heart sank. Had he been reading the same sources as Mrs Hansen, or was her attitude rubbing off on him?

"Not all of them," I said firmly. "Besides, it's just as likely that a human took them."

More, if anything, given that the humans outnumbered the fairies by far… with one obvious exception: Oak. How could I possibly prove the innocence of someone who acted anything but… and did I *want* to?

My gaze landed on the concerned-looking couple at the back of the room, who my paranormal-sensing power instantly identified as a witch and wizard. The man was tall and broad, with the tanned complexion of someone who worked outside a lot, while the woman's features suggested Asian heritage, and I envied her straight, glossy black hair. Since both of them were human, had their daughter been targeted simply because of her proximity to the forest or to Mrs Hansen? Her loud complaints couldn't be helping the situation, but Steve refused to budge and let me into the police station. Instead, I turned away, resigning myself to calling for late-night takeout with Nathan instead of our planned double date at the Troll's Tavern.

Nathan himself didn't talk much until Steve was out of sight. "Looks like Steve didn't want an update from me after all."

"Guess he's occupied with Rhiannon's parents," I said. "They seemed… normal. More so than Mrs Hansen, anyway. Is her ex staying in town?"

"If he is, I hope he's staying at a hotel," came Nathan's response. "He called her behaviour erratic, and I'm inclined to agree."

"Question was, did it start before or after her kid disappeared?" I said. "Because if she's always been this obsessed with the fairies…"

Then was it a simple coincidence that they'd taken her child? No, her ex had said clearly that this was a recent obsession of hers since the fairies' return to the falls.

Had someone been trying to frame the fairies on purpose? Someone like Mrs Hansen herself?

9

After I left work the following day, I went to check up on my dad and the fairies, hoping that Steve and the other gargoyles had listened to Nathan and decided against going back to interrogate them all again. It was far better for them to search the forest and to question people I hadn't used my lie-sensing power on. With the exception, of course, of a certain fairy who'd evaded all attempts to pin him down. I'd have to figure out what to do about him soon and whether keeping his secret was worth risking the safety of the other fairies.

I came to a startled halt when the pixie appeared in a flash of glitter on the path in front of me. "What's up?"

The pixie flew up into the air, beckoning to me with urgent chittering noises. Assuming he wanted to lead me to the forest, I followed him uphill, but instead of heading towards the forest, he veered away towards the university campus instead. Had the posters reappeared again? Or were Rodney and his friends causing more trouble?

I picked up speed until I reached the fence circling the campus, switching to fairy mode and flying over. Part of me expected to find the other fairies hiding in the shadows again, but nobody waited on the other side of the fence. I didn't see any new anti-fairy posters on the sides of the buildings, either, so why had the pixie brought me here? I looked for him, but he'd disappeared somewhere among the maze of buildings.

For the lack of any better ideas, I turned into human mode again and walked to the library, figuring I might as well check in with Samuel while I was there.

The vampire greeted me at the door with a fanged smile. "This is a pleasant surprise, Blair. Can I help you with something?"

"Um…" *I came here because the pixie led me to campus without explaining why.* "I'm looking for more information on the fairies."

"Did you read the last book I loaned you?" he asked.

"Most of it," I said. "I'm not really looking for a guide to fairies, though. I want to see where this children-kidnapping idea originated."

"Ah." He turned towards the shelves. "You'll want the folklore section. The two overlap in some aspects, of course, but like other stories about paranormals written by those without direct experience with our world, there are elements that are entirely fictitious. This way."

The vampire moved among the winding shelves, and I did my best to remember the way back so I wouldn't end up lost in the stacks. He then came to a halt beside a relatively small section marked Folklore. Most of the aged books looked more like they belonged to the normal world than the magical one, which made a kind of sense.

Magical people didn't need to write down fairy tales when they lived the impossible every day.

Sensing Samuel was about to leave me alone to browse, I said, "Did you talk to the other staff about those posters?"

"There was no need," he said. "Someone removed every one of them from campus, so I had no evidence to present to them."

Oops. "But the people who put them up are still recruiting people, aren't they?"

A scowl exposed his fangs. "Yes, but not in a way that can effectively be disciplined. It's frowned upon for me to use my mind-reading powers on the students unless it's necessary."

"Oh." I hadn't considered that issue, but it figured that the people with an irrational obsession with fairies would also throw a fit about a vampire reading their minds. "I just worry about them having more ammunition now that two children have vanished, though, that's all."

"Two?" he said.

"Didn't you hear about the second girl who disappeared yesterday?" Maybe word hadn't made it to campus yet, but it would, no doubt. Soon.

"A second disappearance?" he said. "No, I hadn't heard."

"I helped search the forest for her yesterday," I explained. "She vanished from the same road as the first victim. I'm not sure what's going on over there, to tell you the truth, but it isn't the fairies."

"I'm afraid I haven't been near the forest in some time, Blair, so I have no comment to offer," said the vampire.

"Take your time browsing this section. And try not to get into any more trouble, won't you?"

"I'll try not to." I watched him vanish among the shelves, then I turned back to the array of titles on offer, wishing he'd given me a little more direction. I didn't even know where to start, so I selected a book called *Changelings and Folktales* that looked promising and then stiffened when I heard lowered voices from behind the shelves. Familiar voices—or one of them was, anyway.

"They're even more suspicious than she is," said the voice. "Here, it's this way."

I hastily ducked out of sight between two shelves as Rodney came into view—the guy with the shaved head who'd come to help Mrs Hansen protest against the fairies. Upon realising that the gap in the shelves wasn't much of a hiding place, I swiftly snapped my fingers and turned invisible.

Rodney neared the shelves, accompanied by two other guys I recognised from the group who'd accompanied Mrs Hansen to bother the fairies. "Did you see that?"

"See what?" asked a gangly boy with acne splattered across his nose.

"A weird glittery flash," said Rodney. "It looked like one of *them.*"

"You're getting a little paranoid, Rodney," said the other. "Seeing fairies everywhere."

"Don't speak their names," he hissed. "That's what summons them."

I stifled a laugh, remaining still. He really had taken his fear of fairies to the next level, it seemed, but what was he doing in the folklore section? Nothing good, I assumed.

"C'mon, the book's here," said his friend. "Samuel said."

Rodney walked straight up to the shelf where I'd been standing a minute beforehand. I held my breath, wishing I'd moved further away, but I was too close to risk moving in case I drew their attention. He scanned the shelves, looking more and more annoyed by the second. "It's not here."

"Someone else take it out?" said the pimply guy.

"Or he lied," said Rodney. "Maybe he's the one who removed our posters."

"Does he ever leave the library, though?" said his other friend. "Nah, I bet someone took it out for research. Someone who wants to join us at our demonstration tomorrow morning."

They're holding another demonstration?

"I hope so," he said. "Because if *they* find out, they'll probably turn us into trees, like they did to Mrs Hansen."

Of course she'd told everyone about that incident. Typical. More to the point, I had a faint suspicion that the book they were looking for was in my own hands and that Samuel had sent them to fetch it on purpose.

I remained hidden until they vanished from sight. Then I emerged from between the shelves, my motivation already dimming. I might as well take out the book I'd chosen while I was here, but it seemed nothing would deter Rodney and his friends from hassling the fairies and causing trouble.

Did Samuel know they'd organised another protest? Or the rest of the staff? It wasn't against the rules, as far as I was aware, but the fairies didn't deserve to have their weekend disturbed by Rodney and his gormless friends rampaging around the forest any more than they deserved to be hassled by the police when they hadn't committed any crimes. I wouldn't lie—the idea of Conor turning them all into trees wasn't unappealing—but I doubted that would work in anyone's favour.

I gave Rodney plenty of time to leave the library before turning visible again and selecting a few more books at random. By some miracle, I managed not to get lost on my way to check them out, but Samuel had disappeared somewhere among the shelves, and I didn't want to end up walking in circles to find him while carrying a stack of heavy textbooks. No doubt he was trying to avoid the students himself, so I checked out my books as quickly as possible before cramming them into my bag and leaving the library.

It was only when I left the campus that I remembered the pixie, who'd disappeared from sight long before. Had he known Rodney and his friends were up to no good again? Was that why he'd led me here?"

———

"What on earth are you doing, Blair?" asked Alissa as I entered the living room, struggling under the weight of the newly acquired textbooks in my bag. "Taking on extra magical theory work?"

"Not exactly." I piled the books on the table with a *thunk* that woke Sky. He gave a disgruntled *miaow and pointedly sprawled across my seat.* "I want to see if these fairy tales have any truth buried in them."

"Really?" She picked up the *Changelings and Folklore* book. "I think a normal wrote this one."

"Doesn't make it less viable."

"I know that, Blair," she said. "If the books were

written by normals, though, then they wouldn't have known the difference between reality and myth the way a paranormal would."

"Maybe, but even the magical world has out-of-date and untrue rumours when it comes to the fairies," I said. "Besides, I want to know where Mrs Hansen gets her information."

"The internet, I expect," said Alissa.

"Not just there," I said. "I just saw Rodney and his friends at the library in the same section as me. In fact, I think I took out the same book they were interested in taking for themselves."

"Pity for them." She petted Roald, who lay sprawled on her lap. "Samuel said they were failing all their classes and had nothing better to do with their time. Especially that Rodney, who only got into the university because his mum had important links to the regional witch council and pulled some strings."

"He has a serious case of fairy-related paranoia." I arranged the books into a neater stack. "Worse, he and his mates are planning another protest tomorrow morning. Didn't say where, but I'm guessing the forest."

"I doubt he'll do anything too outrageous," she said. "Especially if the police are around."

"If they even know," I said. "Not sure they do, but I already questioned all the fairies about that missing girl, and it wasn't them. I know Steve didn't necessarily take my word for it, but I'm certain. My lie-sensing power would have reacted if I wasn't."

"Of course," said Alissa. "Don't take this the wrong way, though, but until the missing-persons case is completely resolved, there's not much anyone can do to stop Mrs Hansen from roaming around the forest."

I restacked the textbooks to avoid meeting her eyes. "Nobody deserves to get woken up by that Rodney waving a misspelled poster in their face. Besides, he and his friends are feeding Mrs Hansen's suspicions about her child being kidnapped by a fairy when it might not be based in reality."

Assuming she hadn't manufactured the whole situation herself, of course. The idea had lurked at the back of my mind for the past day, but without proof, I doubted anyone would believe the possibility that Mrs Hansen might have arranged the disappearance of her own child to drive the fairies out of town. I scarcely believed it myself, after all.

One way to see if the idea had any credibility would be to speak to the parents of the second missing child and see if they were the sort who were likely to have opposed the fairies before the incident this week. On a whim, I texted Nathan, asking if he was around. He replied a moment later, saying he was on his way back from work, so I'd timed my query well.

"Date with Nathan?" Alissa guessed, seeing the phone in my hand. "Got to make up for yesterday, right?"

"Yesterday we ordered takeout and watched TV after our trip to the forest, so it wasn't all bad." I reached over and stroked Sky, seeing he was awake. "Besides, I want to see if he has any updates on the missing kids."

Nathan showed up within a few minutes and rang the doorbell. I met him outside, where he greeted me with a customary hug and kiss. "Hey, Blair."

"Hey," I said. "Lucky timing. Did Steve have you combing the forest again?"

"You've got it," he said. "He's at the office, though, so I'm not complaining about getting some peace from his grumbling."

"I wondered if Rhiannon's parents were still around," I said. "At the police station, I mean."

"They might be. Any reason?"

"There's going to be another protest," I admitted. "I overheard the students at the library talking about it. Tomorrow morning."

His brows rose. "You were at the campus library?"

"The pixie led me there, but I'm not sure why," I said. "I talked to Samuel, since I was there, and I got out a few textbooks on fairy folklore. I figured I'd see where Mrs Hansen and the others are getting their information, but I also would like to know if Rhiannon's parents are likely to fall for that kind of thing too."

His lips pressed together. "They *might* be at the police station, but I doubt Steve will be thrilled if I tell him."

"He needs to know, though, right?" I asked. "I know it's not ideal. I didn't know Rodney and his friends were going to show up at the library when they did, but he's got this really weird fixation on fairies. I'm worried he might start trouble if the police aren't there to keep an eye on him."

"I understand," he said. "I can talk to Steve. I can't promise he'll care enough to send anyone to watch though."

"Yeah... I'm not sure if he took my word for it when I told him to leave the fairies alone either," I admitted. "Steve doesn't like being told he's wrong."

"You've got that right," he said. "Tell you what, come with me and we'll talk to him, and then we'll go to the Troll's Tavern to make up for yesterday. Deal?"

"I like the way you think." After waving goodbye to Alissa, I walked with Nathan to the police station. "I hope Mrs Hansen isn't there."

"She shouldn't be," said Nathan. "According to Steve, the police are giving her daily updates, but it's Rhiannon's parents who are the priority at the moment, as their daughter vanished more recently, and they think it's likely that if they find her, it'll lead them straight to Laurel."

"Yeah." Guilt swirled inside me. "Before she vanished, I did wonder if Mrs Hansen was telling the full truth."

"How so?" he said.

"I don't know, but it seems odd that the person who vanished was the child of someone who hates fairies," I said. "It sounds like this is a recent fixation of hers, but she jumped straight to the conclusion that her daughter was taken by fairies. What if she or someone else made it look that way on purpose?"

His brows shot up. "You think someone wanted to frame the fairies for the kidnappings?"

"Don't tell Steve," I added. "I have no proof except for a bunch of textbooks full of stories about fairies kidnapping human children for the fun of it, which doesn't exactly paint a picture of innocence. But you'd think if Mrs Hansen was worried about the fairies in the forest, she wouldn't have left her daughter alone in the garden. The timing seems suspicious. I don't know."

I stopped talking as we neared the police station. Through the doors, I saw Rhiannon's parents were still there, near the back of the lobby, but Mrs Hansen was mercifully nowhere to be seen. As Nathan and I entered, Steve lumbered over to us. "Back *again,* Blair Wilkes? I knew I never should have let you have your way."

"I'm not here to ask for anything," I told him, conscious of Mr and Mrs Bradley's presence in the background. "I heard there's going to be an anti-fairy demonstration tomorrow morning, and I imagine it'll be in the forest like the last one."

"What do you expect me to do about that?" he said. "It's not against the law."

"You aren't worried the students will start trouble like they did last time?" I asked.

"I have better things to do with my time," he said.

"Like finding those two missing children, I hope." I glanced at Rhiannon's parents, who were staring openly at me across the lobby. "Do you have any leads?"

"None," Steve said. "Yet."

I studied Mr and Mrs Bradley, who still registered as nothing more than humans. Before I lost my nerve, I approached them. "I hope I'm not intruding, but I wondered if you'd spoken to Mrs Hansen. Aside from when she was here yesterday, I mean."

"No," said Mrs Bradley. "I heard her, though... she claimed the fairies took her child and told all these stories about fairies capturing human children."

"They're just stories." I should have known they'd have heard her railing against the fairies, considering how much time she'd spent here lately. "I've spoken to every single one of the fairies, and none of them has set eyes on her child or yours. When was the last time you saw her?"

"Get out." Steve shooed me away. "I never said you could do any more questioning, Blair Wilkes. Out."

Worth a shot. I trailed out of the police station, hoping he'd take my concerns about the protest tomorrow seriously enough to at least send one gargoyle to watch out for trouble.

As for Rhiannon's parents, they didn't seem to share Mrs Hansen's irrational fear of fairies based on what I'd seen, but that didn't mean they hadn't listened to her stories. Aside from that, no obvious link existed between the two families.

So who took them, then?

10

Since I couldn't sleep that night, I read through the book I'd borrowed from the library. The array of tales involving the kidnapping of human children did not help me relax, unsurprisingly, while I found myself wondering why the pixie had even led me to the library in the first place. Had he wanted me to find the books? Unlikely, since pixies definitely couldn't read minds, and he'd disappeared shortly after I'd entered the campus. Maybe I should have gone to see my dad instead, to warn him of the upcoming protest in the forest, but I'd have to wait until morning to tell him the bad news.

I read page after page of myth and rumour and tall tale until my eyes grew too heavy to keep open. Tales of children being replaced by magical doppelgängers or spirited away to fairyland danced through my dreams all night and merged with my own experience at the goblin market in a montage of fairy trickery. I woke briefly, dragged to wakefulness by the sound of Nathan leaving the house silently so as not to wake me. Sky happily took over his side of the bed, while I drifted off again.

This time, I dreamt of Oak's house, which, in the typical manner of dream logic had grown to the size of a palace. For a similar reason, I didn't question when I woke up inside a bedroom there and walked out to find a dozen children playing in the corridor.

"What are they doing here?" I asked of nobody in particular.

"They're changelings," said Oak. "They belong here."

I turned to face the fairy, who bared his teeth in a grin. "Why am *I* here?"

"You're a changeling, too, Blair," said my dad.

At the end of the corridor, Mrs Hansen appeared, gave a sneer and a wave, and disappeared. Then a giant furry monster leapt onto my chest.

I jerked awake to find Sky had planted himself on top of me while I was asleep. After wriggling out from underneath him, I showered and dressed alone, and I was on my way downstairs when Nathan returned, closing the front door behind him.

"Hey." I greeted him with a kiss. "Where've you been?"

"Trying to convince Steve to send someone to keep an eye on Rodney and his friends," he said. "Didn't work. I sent Erin instead."

"Miaow," Sky said from the top of the stairs.

"What is it?" I asked. "Do you want to come to keep an eye on Rodney and his friends in the forest?"

"Miaow," Sky said.

"I'd be glad to have him there," said Nathan.

So would I. With Sky capable of shifting into his monster form at any time, it'd be much easier to break up any confrontation before it got out of hand. Of course, my cat turning into a giant beast wouldn't do anything to endear us to Mrs Hansen or the others, but I trusted him not to bring out the monstrous disguise unless he had a very good reason for it.

After a quick breakfast, the two of us headed for the forest, where Sky took the lead along the winding path towards the fairies' home. While I'd worried we might end up being too late, no signs of Rodney or his friends materialised.

"Maybe they won't show up," I remarked as it began to rain, droplets sliding off the leaves and dripping onto our heads. "For all we know, Rodney is a wimp, and he'll call it off because of the weather."

"I doubt rain would deter them," he said. "The fairies can summon up worse."

"Better not say that in front of him or the others."

Not that they didn't know what the fairies were capable of anyway, but their fear had distorted their vision. If they'd been reading the stories from those library books, it'd explain why, but that didn't mean the fairy residents of the forest deserved to deal with the fallout.

The rain grew heavier, sliding off the leaves and forming puddles on the forest floor. Sky sheltered himself under my coat, wriggling between my feet to hide himself from the rain. I was debating heading deeper into the woods when I spotted Rodney and his friends approaching, several of them carrying soggy-looking cardboard signs. Mrs Hansen occupied a prominent position and was waving a large sign saying, No More Fairies. At least her spelling was an improvement on Rodney's.

As they advanced, my dad came to stand alongside Nathan and me. Then Sky positioned himself in front of us, growling, which brought the whole procession to a halt.

"You," Mrs Hansen said to me. "Get out of the way."

"You're blocking our path," said Rodney.

"*MIAOW*," Sky said, so loudly that Rodney tripped backwards over his own feet and nearly dropped his sign.

"That's no normal cat," he proclaimed.

"That's Sky," I said. "I wouldn't insult him if I were you. He says you should leave."

"This is a residential area," said Nathan. "You're welcome to take your protest elsewhere in the city. The high street, for instance."

"Get out of the way," Rodney repeated, though there was less heat in his voice than before. "Weren't you a hunter? You shouldn't be supporting those freaks."

Nathan rarely lost his temper, but I was glad not to be on the receiving end of the steely expression on his face. "I'm head of Fairy Falls's security team. If you don't want me to report you to the police, I'd rethink your choices."

"This *is* a residential area," my dad added. "Disturbing the peace isn't allowed, Rodney, according to the laws set out by the Meadowsweet Coven."

I hadn't known he'd been reading up on the covens' laws, but it made sense that he'd want to have that information to hand in case anyone kicked up a fuss about the fairies' return to town.

Rodney just gawped at us, apparently lost for words, but Mrs Hansen was less convinced.

"We came here because our children were taken by the residents in this forest," she said. "My useless husband has already left town. He's given up on her, but I won't. I won't!"

Rodney and some of the others murmured agreement, but from the nature of their signs, it was pretty clear that they cared more about driving the fairies off than about finding Laurel Hansen. The question was, how much of her own outrage was for show too?

"I was just pointing out that these people aren't interested in finding Laurel," I said, indicating Rodney and his friends. "If you want results, you'd be better served working with the police instead."

"The police aren't doing enough," she insisted. "They're on the side of the monsters living here in this forest."

"I don't see them anywhere," I said. "Besides, I spoke to the fairies and verified that none of them has seen Laurel *or* Rhiannon."

At that moment, Rodney made the mistake of trying to step forward, only for Sky to bat the cardboard sign out of his hand with one swipe of his paw.

"*MIAOW,*" Sky said.

"Can't you shut that animal up?" Rodney retrieved the sign and pulled out his wand, pointing directly at Sky.

"Absolutely not." All semblance of civility shattered. "If you lay a finger on my cat, I *will* call the police. What did you intend to do when you reached the fairies' part of the forest?"

"Nothing," said Rodney.

Lie. I didn't need my lie-sensing power to know that was nonsense. They'd come here with a purpose, after all.

"I doubt that to be true," my dad said. "If you simply wanted to express your views, then you could have gone elsewhere and achieved the same result. You came here to disturb the residents, who have already been questioned by the police and verified as innocent of the two children's disappearances."

"They're liars and tricksters," she spat. "They capture human children. All the stories say that."

"That," I said, "is a rumour made up by normals as a cautionary tale. You're witches and wizards. You should know better than to believe stories told to frighten children."

Mrs Hansen's face turned brick red. "They aren't just stories. The things we've seen... this part of the forest doesn't even *exist*."

"Being different doesn't mean being dangerous." I glanced at Rodney, my heart sinking when I saw him raise his wand.

I moved to deflect his spell, but before he could finish casting, Rodney's wand transformed into a snake. Rodney yelped, dropping the serpent, only for it to transform into a wand again when it hit the ground. I glimpsed the faintest movement from my dad to clue me in that he'd cast the spell, but several of the others pulled their wands out as Rodney scrambled to retrieve his own from the mud.

"Freak," Rodney growled.

Before anyone else could cast any spells, Nathan stepped in. "That was a hostile spell, Rodney. If you want to avoid being charged by the police, I'd suggest you leave the forest immediately. All of you."

"You heard my brother." Erin stepped into view, along with Buck and some of the other security team members. Even Rob came to join them, so I assumed the werewolves had been watching the situation too.

Seeing they were outnumbered, Rodney and the others had no choice but to let themselves be escorted from the forest. Once Nathan had left, only my dad and I were left behind, with Sky sitting at our feet.

"Miaow," he growled after the students' retreating backs, which probably meant *Don't come back.*

I drew in a breath and faced my dad. "They don't actually care about finding the missing children. If anything, it's more helpful for their cause if they *don't* find them."

"I don't doubt that," Dad said darkly. "Short of the police agreeing to ban them from their gatherings, though, I'm not sure there's a permanent way to stop them from coming here."

"I guess not." My shoulders slumped. "I'm not convinced Steve is doing all he can to find those kids, either, but there's got to be another way to handle this."

"I hope we've shown them that they won't be unopposed if they come here again, in any case," he said.

"I liked your trick with Rodney's wand," I said. "I never thought of using glamour like that."

"Fairy magic might not be as varied as witch magic, but it can be versatile."

"I never thought it wasn't," I clarified. "I'd like to learn more, but I feel like I'm failing at being both a witch *and* a fairy lately."

"I don't believe that's true," he responded. "You're doing the best you can with a lot of responsibility."

"Still." I glanced over my shoulder, wondering if the other fairies were watching us from a distance. "I can't help but feel like I've broken trust with the fairies by questioning them the way I did. I hoped it'd stop Mrs Hansen from coming back, but it didn't work."

"You haven't broken their trust," he said firmly. "They know the circumstances are less than ideal and are willing to be patient until the missing children are found."

"Yeah." I fidgeted. "It's not just that. I promised Rosalyn and Ani I'd help them find employment, but it's harder than I expected. So many employers have the requirement that their clients need to be able to use a wand."

"Have you talked to them about what they want?"

"I did, but…" I hesitated. "I thought I might suggest they join the town's security team, but considering they'd have to work in close proximity to Steve, that might not be the best idea."

"It can't hurt to ask," he said. "This tense state of affairs won't last forever. Fairies' skills are well suited to that kind of work."

I guess they are. Buck had settled in in no time at all, and I could picture Rosalyn and Ani having a field day throwing glitter at potential trespassers. Far more than I could picture either of them stacking shelves, anyway. But until the situation with Mrs Hansen and the others cooled down, I might have to shelve that idea.

"I guess," I said. "The problem is that I don't know where they might fit in, because *I* don't fit in. I never really fit anywhere in the normal world either. Being the magical world's misfit isn't easy."

"You've made friends, though," said Dad. "I thought you were happy here."

"I am," I insisted. "I just wish… it's ridiculous, but I thought that after we got rid of the hunters and Mrs

Dailey was in jail, it'd bring an end to this kind of strife. I shouldn't have expected the others to welcome the fairies with open arms, but still."

The hunters were disdainful at best towards paranormals as a whole, so I'd come to expect it of them and from witches like Mrs Dailey too. Yet seeing the other paranormals turn on the newcomers had hurt far more than I'd expected.

"It's not irrational at all," he said. "I hoped we'd have a smoother ride too. I think when the two children are found, though, we'll be able to put these issues behind us."

"Assuming they do show up," I said. "Rodney and the others don't seem to care either way. All they want is an excuse to make trouble, and this situation gave them exactly what they were looking for."

He arched a brow. "Are you implying Rodney and his friends might have manufactured Laurel Hansen's disappearance on purpose?"

"The thought did come to mind," I admitted. "I should have tried out my lie-sensing power on *them*, but I'm not sure whether Mrs Hansen was involved herself."

"You think Mrs Hansen handed her child off to someone else?" he queried. "Wasn't there an ex-husband?"

"Oh." I clapped a hand to my mouth. "I never thought of that. He said he hadn't seen her in ages, though, and he didn't lie. That doesn't mean he wasn't involved, but if he's left town, then we might be too late to question him again."

I hadn't questioned *him* in depth except by verifying he hadn't seen his daughter recently, but there was the odd way my paranormal-sensing powers had reacted to him.

Or rather, not reacted. What if that wasn't all he was hiding?

Sky meowed and shook water off his furry coat, soaking my shoes. "I think he's trying to tell me to get out of the rain. I should go and find Nathan, but I wish I could do something else to help the fairies."

"You might have another chance tomorrow," he remarked. "Madame Grey is holding a council meeting tomorrow for the leaders of the town's paranormal communities, and I'm invited to attend on behalf of the fairies if I so desire. At the meeting, I will bring up the recent events and ask the witches whether the police should be doing more to protect them."

My mouth dropped open. "Seriously?"

I'd forgotten the incident last year when I'd shown up at a council meeting, representing the fairies in order to make myself heard, though at the time, I'd been the only one in town. If I showed up with my dad, the witches would have twice the reason to listen to the fairies' concerns, but that didn't mean they'd do anything about Rodney and his troublemaking friends.

"Yes, I think it's a good idea for me to make my thoughts plain in front of the coven leaders," he said. "I personally think we need at least one fairy on the council to ensure our voices are heard."

"Is that why you've been reading up on the covens' laws?" I asked.

"Of course," he said. "I know the town better than the other new arrivals, though I missed many years and was never a permanent resident like you are."

"You are now," I said. "Rodney and the others won't be

able to take that away from you. Nor from the others either."

I sounded more confident than I really felt, but I'd need to be in top form if I wanted to convince the council to listen to us.

My dad squeezed my shoulder. "I'm proud of everything you've achieved so far, Blair. Don't doubt that for an instant."

"I wish it felt like enough."

Talking to the council would be a starting point, though there was a small chance some of Mrs Dailey's former supporters would also be there... and *they'd* certainly have a reason to want the fairies gone. After all, they'd also supported the hunters, who'd come close to doing exactly that.

Yet my dad intended to turn up to the meeting despite knowing some of them would have been happy to let him stay in jail for the duration of his lifelong sentence. He was far braver than I was, that was for sure. The least I could do was show up as backup and say what I needed to.

I normally slept in late on Sundays, but no matter how hard I tried, I couldn't drift off. I ended up reading my way through the books I'd borrowed from the library until fiction blurred with reality and yet another dream of fairies and changelings and monsters invaded my thoughts.

Sky woke me from my unpleasant nightmares by walking over my face, prompting me to turn over with a shiver.

Nathan tilted his head to look at me. "Can't sleep?"

I shook my head. Sky meowed and shoved his way between us, demanding a stroke. I gave him one, propping myself up on my elbow. "I said I'd go to the witches' council meeting today, and now I can't stop thinking about it."

"Want me to go with you?"

I shook my head. "You should help Steve look for the missing girls. Or keep him away from the fairies. Rodney and the others too. It wouldn't surprise me if they tried another protest while they knew the witches were occupied with the council meeting."

"You might have a point there."

I'd told Nathan about my new theory that Mrs Hansen might have handed her kid off to her ex-husband for safekeeping before pretending fairies had taken her, but it would be difficult to find any proof. For a start, I wasn't sure she'd ever told an outright lie. I probably should have asked her more questions, but it hadn't occurred to me that she might have gone so far as to make her own child disappear in order to blame the fairies for it.

Then there was the way my paranormal-sensing powers had lacked any reaction to Pierce, which I couldn't explain at all. So far, the only people they hadn't worked on were powerful fairies and the dead. I was fairly sure Pierce wasn't a ghost, which left the former option. If he was secretly a fairy, it might go some way to explaining where Mrs Hansen had acquired such a grudge against them, but that didn't seem quite right either. And he hadn't lied when he'd claimed not to have seen his daughter since long before she'd disappeared.

Either way, I wouldn't be able to announce that particular theory at the meeting without seeming unhinged, so I'd need to figure out a way to tease out more proof beforehand.

After showering and dressing, I left Nathan's house for the council meeting. Sky declined to come with me by means of pretending to be asleep, but he wouldn't be able to do much in this particular situation. Turning into a giant beast in the middle of the council meeting would not be as useful as it'd been in the forest.

I met my dad outside the witches' headquarters. While

this would be his first council meeting, he seemed a lot calmer than me. I was a bundle of jittery nerves, unable to keep from fidgeting.

"Ready?" he asked.

I nodded. "I hope so."

Vincent the vampire approached and halted in front of my dad, extending a hand. "I don't believe we've met."

"Braden Eventide," said my dad, shaking hands with the vampire. "You're Vincent the Elder, correct?"

"Correct," said the vampire. "I've heard a lot about you. Especially from Blair's cat."

He spoke loudly enough for one of the nearby witches to give me a baffled look. My dad, however, wasn't fazed. "I suspect everyone here has heard enough about me to form their own opinions. I came here in an attempt to set the record straight."

Yeah. I just hope your past in jail doesn't come back to bite both of us. Mrs Dailey had attempted to use my dad's imprisonment against me inside a council meeting herself, in fact, but without my dad actually being there as a witness.

Now that I thought about it, Vincent hadn't learned about my dad just from reading my cat's thoughts. He'd probably known Dad's ancestors too. The vampire hadn't exactly been forthcoming about just how much he *did* know, but before either of us could ask any more questions, Madame Grey herself opened the door to the witches' headquarters and beckoned us after her through a door into the council room.

"Do come in," she said over her shoulder.

The rest of us filed into the council room behind her, taking our places at the long table dominating the room.

The vast majority of the coven leaders were witches, since coven leadership was typically matrilineal. Rita sat among the other leaders of the town's most prominent witch covens, of which there'd been some changes since the last meeting I'd attended, but that was to be expected after Madame Grey had made some restructuring efforts following Mrs Dailey's attempted coup.

Also present was Rebecca, the Head Witch, who smiled in my direction from near Madame Grey. Everyone else's attention was fixed on my dad, however, and their expressions ranged from intrigued to wary. Since nobody else seemed inclined to sit next to Vincent the vampire, I took a seat on his right, with my dad on my other side. Chief Donovan of the pack was notably absent, while the Elf King never came to council meetings anyway.

When the table was almost full, Madame Grey called the meeting to start. "We have a new council member present today."

"I am Braden Eventide," said my father, while everyone turned in his direction. "I once lived here in Fairy Falls, but I spent some time away before I decided to move back to be closer to my daughter."

Everyone in the room knew exactly where he'd been, but nobody said so aloud, despite a murmur travelling along the length of the table and coming to an abrupt halt when Vincent gave everyone a fanged smile.

"Let us begin," said Madame Grey. "We have a few issues on the table this morning. To start with, the fairies have requested an extension to their territory in the forest. The elves refused to cede any of their own territory to them, as did the werewolves."

"So we're supposed to give up ours instead?" asked one of the witches, while several others muttered among themselves.

"Not at all," said Madame Grey. "Through the use of glamour, or illusion, there is no need for any of us to give up our own part of the forest. It's my understanding that the fairies simply requested that we allow them to create another path out of their own territory."

"Correct," my father said. "That way, they will be able to get in and out without trespassing in your part of the woods… or the elves' or shifters'.'"

"I think that seems reasonable," said Madame Grey. "We can talk specifics later. Does anyone object?"

Nobody made any complaints.

"Next," said Madame Grey. There's also been a request to update our textbooks on the history of the town. Everyone knows the story of the origin of Fairy Falls but not its true and extensive one."

My heart jolted in my chest as she glanced at me. Rita must have told her about my comments during our lesson, and perhaps she thought I'd attended the meeting for that reason. Unfortunately, I'd forgotten all about it, and my mind helpfully went blank when faced with an audience.

"Does anyone know the full story?" said one of the other witches. "Aside from the oldest of the vampires, I imagine nobody here would have lived long enough to remember."

Oak did. Not that he'd be volunteering to educate anyone, but there was no denying that the fairies were better equipped to give their side of the story. I had an inkling, though, that even the most open-minded witches would object to a bunch of apparent strangers writing over the history they'd been teaching for generations.

"Nevertheless," said Madame Grey, "I think it's worth revisiting the story in light of recent events… particularly the town's original inhabitants' return."

"Oh, really?" a voice rang out across the room. "You really want to spread the lies of the fairies and poison the minds of our children?"

All eyes went to the door as none other than Mrs Hansen sailed into the room, a notebook tucked under her arm and her eyes narrowed in disapproval at the sight of my father and me sitting there at the table. Regardless, she pulled out a chair and sat down herself, glowering at everyone up and down the table until Madame Grey cleared her throat.

"Welcome, Mrs Hansen. I confess I am somewhat surprised to see you here, since you're not the leader of a coven."

"Perhaps not, but I have concerns that I strongly believe need to be heard," she said.

"Oh?" said Madame Grey. "Do enlighten me on what you mean by that."

Why are you giving her the chance to speak?

Mrs Hansen's eyes gleamed with satisfaction upon finding herself with a captive audience. "I'm here representing a number of fellow citizens who oppose the beasts and tricksters moving into the forest. From the sounds of things, I got here just in time, since you seem to be considering allowing these newcomers to rewrite our own history."

"Not at all," said Madame Grey. "You misunderstand, Mrs Hansen. We simply intend to give our history textbooks a much-needed update in light of new information. It's certainly not unheard of."

Despite her confident tone, several of the witches had begun to whisper among themselves while stealing glances at Mrs Hansen… and at my dad and me.

"Perhaps not," said Mrs Hansen. "I do have to question the timing, given how little experience these newcomers have of the magical world as a whole. Though I'm sure the covens themselves are in need of an update. One might even suggest they've outlived their usefulness and ought to be replaced by a new system instead."

I'd heard *that* before… from Mrs Dailey, Rebecca's mother, who'd conspired to put the hunters in charge of the covens. If not for the fact that I knew Mrs Dailey to be locked in a secure cell, I'd have checked to see if Mrs Hansen wasn't the other witch in disguise. Rebecca, clearly thinking the same, tightened her grip on the sceptre until her knuckles whitened.

Madame Grey's gaze was flinty. "I disagree."

She couldn't seriously have come in here expecting everyone to agree with disbanding the covens, could she? Most of the people in this very room had witnessed Mrs Dailey's arrest, for a start. Not to mention the moment when Inquisitor Hare had been exposed as a fairy himself. Had she forgotten that or simply decided to forget that the hunters had been ruled by the fairies she feared so much?

"I simply wanted to ask if the covens are doing any good for the citizens of the town," she said. "Many of us feel our concerns are going unheard. Did you *ask* us if we wanted those strangers moving to town?"

"If you mean my fellow fairies, we were the original

inhabitants of this town," said my dad. "Would you ask the same question of any new witches or wizards who opted to move here? The majority of us have no desire for strife with humans."

"That is enough," Madame Grey said, cutting through Mrs Hansen's objection. "We are not here to debate whether the fairies should be allowed to live here. This is their home."

"What about that other fairy, then?" said Mrs Hansen. "The strange outsider who's been hiding here without telling the covens?"

An unpleasant jolt hit my chest. *Please tell me she doesn't know about Oak.*

"This is the first I'm hearing of such a fairy," Madame Grey said. "Might you tell me how you know there someone living in the forest who has yet to make themselves known to me?"

"I saw him," said Mrs Hansen. "He doesn't live with the others. He hides himself away in a secret place... but *they* know where he is." She pointed straight at my dad and me.

"Is this true?" asked one of the witches.

"Yes," said my dad. "It's true."

Horror crashed over me as he confirmed Mrs Hansen's words. It'd been inevitable that Oak would be exposed eventually, but I'd thought nobody else had seen him show his face outside of his hiding spot. Despite his excursion near the lake the other day, I'd thought he was too clever for that. How long had Mrs Hansen known?

Madame Grey's gaze slid to my face, and I wished I could sink through the chair and into the floor.

I licked my lips. "Um, I saw him, but I don't know how

long he's been living in the forest. I thought he might be like Conor, who's been here for years without any contact with the witches. It didn't matter with him, did it?"

"Conor's circumstances were different," said Madame Grey. "He lived here when the hunters were more powerful and there was a significant danger of them targeting him. Now, without that threat, all fairies ought to feel safe to disclose their presence."

"Safe?" said Mrs Hansen. "We're the ones who are rendered unsafe by their presence, especially our children."

"Oak feels the same as Conor did," I blurted before Mrs Hansen could win anyone else to her side. "For a lot of the fairies, the fear of the hunters coming back hasn't really gone away, and no matter how hard I tried, I couldn't convince him to show his face. It doesn't help that Rodney and the others have been marching around the forest and protesting against the fairies being there. You can't expect him to feel welcome after seeing that, can you?"

"Nevertheless, I will have to pay him a visit in due course," said Madame Grey. "Does anyone else have any issues to raise?"

Nobody did, and while my dad and I had already said our piece, Mrs Hansen had achieved exactly what she wanted. As the meeting ended, the others began to file out of the room. I, however, remained behind to speak to Madame Grey.

When the room was empty, I approached her. "I was telling the truth. Oak was hiding in the forest, but he doesn't trust the witches. That doesn't mean he did anything wrong."

"Blair." Madame Grey shook her head. "I don't doubt you speak true, but you've put me in a difficult position. Mrs Hansen now has a good reason to accuse the fairies of deception."

"Hiding out of fear of being driven off by a bunch of angry witches isn't the same as kidnapping human children," I pointed out.

"You're right, but not everyone will see it that way, especially given Mrs Hansen's claims."

I opened and closed my mouth, trying to think of a delicate way to suggest that Mrs Hansen had carefully timed her revelation about Oak so it'd have the most impact. "Maybe, but I find it odd that she waited until now to tell everyone he's here. If she was truly concerned, wouldn't she have told you or one of the other witches in confidence? I find it hard to believe she learned about him right before a meeting that would enable her to make the fairies look bad in front of an audience."

"If you're suggesting she waited for the opportunity to announce his presence, I suspect you are right," she said. "But there's no proof, and it doesn't absolve Oak of any wrongdoing. He should have told me he was here."

"I tried to convince him to tell you," I said. "I even took Buck with me, hoping another fairy might be able to convince him, but he wouldn't budge."

"I will speak to him myself, as I said," she said. "Your father is waiting for you outside. I suggest you join him."

Dismissed, I left the room, where I spotted Vincent crossing the lobby. Since I knew he could move much faster than I could, I could only assume he wanted to speak to me, so I caught up to him.

"Blair," he said. "I can always trust you to make a council meeting more entertaining."

"Hey, it wasn't me who interrupted by trying to accuse a bunch of innocent people of kidnapping and threatening the peace," I said indignantly. "Did you read Mrs Hansen's thoughts?"

All my theories about Mrs Hansen's motives were just that: theories. And so they would remain until she came into contact with someone who could see into her innermost thoughts… like Vincent, for instance.

"Why would I intrude on her thoughts?" he said.

"Because she's hiding something." I dropped my voice. "I don't think anything she said at the meeting today was accidental. Including telling everyone about Oak."

"I thought you could sense truth from lie, Blair."

"I can, but there's a limit," I said. "Reading minds is something else entirely. Did you hear anything from her that drew your suspicions?"

He paused for a long moment. "Nothing. She hid her thoughts from me somehow."

My mouth fell open. "Why didn't you tell me?"

"I'm telling you now."

"Vincent." I shook my head. "You know that's not what I meant. The other witches ought to know she's deceiving them in plain sight."

"Hiding one's thoughts doesn't mean one is guilty," he said. "I'll see you soon, Blair."

Then he was gone, as if he hadn't given me a jarring reminder of the last time we'd both seen someone use magical means to hide their thoughts. Specifically, that had been a member of the regional witch council who'd secretly supported the hunters and had helped see to my dad's arrest and imprisonment. She'd hidden her thoughts to avoid her motives being exposed.

As for Mrs Hansen? She'd purposely exposed Oak's presence in the forest... but for how long had she known he was there? Did *he* know she knew? He was skilled enough at glamour that his decision to show his face in front of me had been a calculated move, but now a new suspicion began to take shape in my mind.

Mrs Hansen believed the fairies were untrustworthy and capricious, and Oak pretty much defined those qualities, from what I'd seen. The notion of her learning of his presence and keeping it hidden for this long made little sense.

Unless he was in on the plan.

Unless *Oak* had taken the children captive... but with the full intention of acting as a willing scapegoat for Mrs Hansen's attempts to drive the fairies out of town.

Was that why he kept rebuffing anyone who tried to talk to him? It was a stretch, I'd admit, but knowing Mrs Hansen had kept Oak's presence quiet only made sense if both were mutually aware, unless Oak cared so little for humans that the notion of the covens finding out didn't bother him. If Madame Grey paid him a visit... well, we'd see if she had any more luck talking to him than I had.

My dad approached me, shaking me out of my reverie. "Blair, we should leave. Do you want to come with me to see the other fairies?"

"You mean Oak?" I said. "I hope you know how to tell him he'll be getting a visit from the coven, because it's going to happen sooner rather than later."

"I confess I didn't expect to have so much trouble convincing him to speak to them," he said. "Or that Mrs

Hansen would learn he was here before he showed his face."

"Mrs Hansen already knew for a while, I'm sure," I said. "She waited until now to tell everyone for maximum impact."

"Are you sure?" he said. "It doesn't seem plausible that she'd keep his presence quiet given her claims."

"You wouldn't think so," I said, "but that's not all she lied about."

"What else?" he queried.

"She's blocking her thoughts from being read by vampires," I said in an undertone. "The last person who did that ended up being arrested for conspiring with the hunters to get you arrested. Vincent seems to think it doesn't necessarily indicate any wrongdoing, but why would she block her thoughts unless she had something to hide?"

"No, you're right." He walked out of the witches' headquarters, and I followed close behind him. "It certainly indicates she planned her timing well, at the very least."

Was that all she planned, though?

Her actions seemed far too calculated, but how deep did her plotting go? Would she, like Mrs Dailey, work hand in hand with some of the fairies she claimed to hate in order to drive away the rest of them? Or had I let Mrs Dailey's scheming colour my views of every other calculating witch who crossed my path?

As the doors to the witches' headquarters closed behind us, the pixie flitted into view, beating his wings urgently.

"What's he saying?" I asked my dad.

"Mrs Hansen," he said. "She's on her way to the forest right this instant."

"Oh, no," I said. "She's not going to try to provoke Oak before Madame Grey gets there, is she?"

Or confirm that they were working together? If the former, I was less than convinced he wouldn't retaliate in a way that would justify all her fears about fairies being terrifying monsters. If the latter... I didn't even want to think of what the pair of them might achieve if they joined forces against the covens.

I had to get there before she did.

12

I broke into a run, bringing out my wings as I did so. My dad did likewise, and while we were both faster than Mrs Hansen, she had a head start on us. If she got lost in the forest, it would slow her down, but it seemed she'd been spending more time in there than any of us knew.

"She's been planning this," I gasped out as we flew alongside one another. "She knew Oak was hiding, yet she waited until now to accuse him of kidnapping her child, even though he fits all the criteria more than the other fairies do."

"Criteria?" he said.

"You know what I mean." I slowed down to avoid crashing into a tree. "He doesn't like humans, attacks anyone who goes near his house, and is secretive. We saw him wandering around the forest alone, too, when those kids were missing. Why didn't I figure it out sooner?"

"He didn't take them, Blair," said Dad. "I know he's not pleasant to outsiders, but he wouldn't have any reason to capture human children and draw any unnecessary attention."

"Maybe not, but I'm sure he knows Mrs Hansen figured out he was here."

Either way, Mrs Hansen seemed as adept at pretending to be something she wasn't as any fairy. She'd been manipulating the facts since the instant her daughter had vanished, and what better way to manufacture a fake kidnapping than to get an actual fairy involved? It was the perfect setup. Nobody would suspect a thing. Oak also wouldn't be the first fairy who would willingly have exiled themselves from their own kind in order to get revenge on the humans who'd driven them out, even if it meant allying with another human.

We flew to a halt as we reached the part of the forest in which Oak's house was hidden. It didn't look as though Mrs Hansen had made it here first, at least, but tension gripped me with every step.

"We have to be careful," I said in a low voice. "He probably has more traps ready for when someone inevitably comes to confront him. Even if he didn't know Mrs Hansen planned to reveal his location at the meeting today, he'll be ready."

"I really don't think he did, Blair," he said. "I doubt he'd have consented to sit aside if he knew."

"I know it sounds absurd," I acknowledged. "But if she already knew he was here, there's no reason for her not to have confronted him in person the way she did with the others. I'm not sure she's even focused on finding her daughter anymore."

Dad shot me a frown. "I wouldn't say that, Blair. Her daughter's disappearance was the catalyst."

"Or so she wants us to think," I said. "I'm not saying she doesn't care for Laurel at all, but I find it hard to believe at least some of her crusade wasn't planned."

Not that I had any proof, since she'd blocked even the elder vampire from reading her thoughts.

His brows shot up. "You think she arranged to have her own child kidnapped… by a fairy?"

"Like I said… it sounds absurd until you look at the evidence." I picked up the pace. "If I were her and I wanted to turn everyone against the fairies by making a deal with one of them, I'd pick him. Can you imagine any of the other fairies cooperating with her?"

"No," he allowed, "but I can't see Oak working with any humans. Even her."

"Not even if it ends with the other fairies leaving and the covens being replaced?" I asked. "You weren't here when Mrs Dailey tried to do something similar and replace the covens with the hunters, but it's giving me major flashbacks."

"The hunters are no threat any longer, Blair," he said. "I can promise you that."

I wished I could be as certain, yet their ideas seemed to be alive and well if Mrs Hansen and her allies were any indication. "Even if I'm wrong, Oak *did* conceal his presence here. And if he raises a fuss when Madame Grey comes here…"

"Then all the fairies might suffer the backlash." He closed his eyes for a brief moment. "We'd better hope it doesn't come to that."

"She was wearing something that stopped her mind from being read by vampires," I added. "I'd say that proves she had something major to hide."

We rounded a corner, finding that Oak's toadstool-shaped house sat underneath an ominous-looking thundercloud. I approached warily, using my wings to hover above the ground in case another pit appeared beneath my feet. Yet even when I reached the doorstep, no booby traps struck. Weird... and possibly a sign that he'd known Mrs Hansen would reveal his presence at the meeting today. He'd anticipated a visit—but from whom?

I rapped on the door with my knuckles, and I wasn't particularly surprised when nobody answered.

"Oak?" I called.

"Go away," returned the fairy's muffled voice.

"Come out," I said. "We want to talk to you."

"Give me one good reason not to turn you into a tree," he responded.

"Because Mrs Hansen just revealed your existence to the entire witch council, and I thought I'd come and warn you before she shows up first."

The door swung open, revealing the scowling fairy. "What have you done?"

"I've done nothing," I said. "I even gave you the chance to tell the witch council yourself that you were here. Instead, Mrs Hansen found out somehow and told them herself."

His green eyes glittered with fury, while his body faintly glowed around the edges as the air crackled with his building magic. "If anyone dares to trespass into my house, they will not find themselves unchallenged."

"They won't go into your house," I said, trying to keep the tremor out of my voice. "Unless you have something to hide."

"What are you implying?" he said. "Do you think you have the right to invade my home, human?"

My dad stepped in. "We came here to warn you of a potential visit from the coven and to advise you not to attack them if you want to be able to stay here peacefully. Nothing more."

"Perhaps, then, I will not stay here any longer," he said. "Or perhaps I will unleash my wrath upon this town and everyone in it."

"That won't be necessary." As he moved, I glimpsed the glowing tint of a glamour covering the inside of his house. What else might he be hiding in there?

Not the missing children?

Oak glared at me. "What are you looking at, human?"

"Did you know Mrs Hansen figured out you were here?" Panic made my words rush together. "Is there a reason you're still hiding?"

My dad nudged me from behind, a warning look on his face. I tilted my head and spotted none other than Mrs Hansen herself approaching the fairy's house. So much for avoiding a major confrontation between the pair of them.

"You again?" she said. "I've had enough of your interference, Blair Wilkes."

Maybe I'd had it wrong and they weren't allies after all, but when Oak didn't react to her presence, my suspicions returned in full force. While my instincts urged me to run, turning my back on the two of them was out of the question. "Interfering with what? Madame Grey already said she intended to come here to visit Oak. Why are you here if not to cause trouble?"

"Do you think I've forgotten these inhuman beasts

captured my daughter?" she spluttered. "I will not listen to your lies."

"*What* did you call me?" Oak advanced on Mrs Hansen, momentarily exposing the inside of the house. The shimmer of glamour covered the entire house, but from this angle, I could see the individual threads forming it.

Mrs Hansen lifted her wand, while Oak's hands crackled with energy. Meanwhile, I did the only thing I could think of: I snapped my fingers and unravelled the threads of the illusion covering Oak's house.

The fairy made a noise of outrage as the illusion slid away, leaving nothing but an abandoned-looking shack in place of the toadstool-shaped house. I didn't see any signs of Laurel or Rhiannon inside, but by now, I hadn't expected to.

Oak turned on me with a furious expression on his face—but Mrs Hansen recovered from her shock and waved her wand.

"Stop!" Dad ran between them and took the brunt of Mrs Hansen's attack. Her spell sent him sprawling back, ropes wrapping around his arms and legs.

"Hey!" I waved my wand and removed the ropes, allowing my dad to climb to his feet.

Then a bright glow bathed the area, and the toadstool house reappeared in place of the shack. Oak swiftly vanished inside it, slamming the door shut behind him.

Dad barred Mrs Hansen from following him. "Enough."

"He won't be able to stay hidden for long." She wore an expression of defiance. "I'll drag him out into the open even if the coven won't."

"You'll do no such thing," said Dad.

I was wrong. The two weren't working together at all, Mrs Hansen's daughter was still missing, and Oak had twice as many reasons to be furious at the witches as he had earlier. To top it all off, Madame Grey would find him in a raging mood when she showed up here. We had to at least convince Mrs Hansen to leave beforehand.

"You don't have the authority to order anyone to leave the town," I said to Mrs Hansen. "Madame Grey can handle him herself, but she's not going to force anyone to leave. Unless you really do think he kidnapped your daughter, but we both know you don't."

"He's a trickster who hides behind lies." She gestured at the house. "As are you."

"Then why are you carrying a charm that prevents your mind from being read by vampires?" I asked her. "That doesn't make you look very transparent."

Her face turned bright red. "You asked a vampire to read my mind?"

"I didn't need to ask. Vampires always know when someone's hiding their thoughts." Not a very subtle evasion, but I'd been suspicious of her long before Vincent's revelation.

"If you ask me, it's invasive," she muttered.

"Come again?" I said. "I thought you wanted to get rid of the fairies, not create new laws to ban whichever kinds of magic you personally dislike."

Maybe she'd turn on vampires next. People like her were never satisfied, and while I'd guessed wrong about her conspiring with Oak, she was as scheming as Mrs Dailey had been.

My dad moved to my side. "Let us clear up this misunderstanding. It's clear that Laurel is not here, which means you have no reason to be near Oak's house."

"No reason?" she echoed. "I want him gone."

"Isn't your child more of a priority?" I said. "I was wrong to accuse you of working with him, but you can't deny that your priorities seem pretty skewed."

Her face flushed again. "I am making the town safer for everyone by getting rid of these invaders."

"Nobody is getting rid of anyone," said a voice.

Madame Grey. The leader of the Meadowsweet Coven strode over to us, her expression calm as she took in the sight of Mrs Hansen facing off against Dad and me on Oak's doorstep.

"Mrs Hansen came here in an attempt to drive Oak out of his home," said Dad. "I believe you're here to pay him a visit?"

"This is the fairy who has yet to register his presence in town?" she said.

"Yes," I said. "But... he's in a foul mood, and it's my fault."

"Yes, it is," Mrs Hansen said sourly.

I shot her a warning look, and Madame Grey's gaze flickered in her direction. I tensed, half expecting Oak to unleash his magic on her as she approached the door and knocked.

No response came from within.

Dad stepped away from the house. "Mrs Hansen, Madame Grey will handle Oak. Leave it alone."

Her angry gaze passed between us. "This is not over between us, Blair Wilkes. I *will* have my way."

She turned on her heel and strode away, leaving Oak's

house behind. Dad and I waited for a long moment, but she didn't come back. Nor did Oak answer the door.

I caught Madame Grey's eye, and she shook her head at me. "Leave, Blair. I will handle this."

"I'll stay," Dad said. "You should leave."

Humiliation burned my cheeks as I heard the implied end of that sentence—*before you make it worse.*

Already, I'd ruined all chances of Oak trusting any of us, given Mrs Hansen yet more incentive to target the other fairies, and on top of that, the entire council knew my dad and I had concealed the existence of another fairy. I couldn't stay here without making things worse, though, so I left Oak's house and walked alone into the forest.

The last thing I wanted to do was to go home and admit my humiliation to Nathan and Alissa and everyone else. Nor the other fairies, either, though I did check to make sure Mrs Hansen hadn't gone straight to their part of the forest upon her departure. Then I kept walking without any particular plan. Who knew, maybe if I walked for long enough, I might stumble upon the missing children. I was out of any better ideas, after all.

Movement stirred at the side of the path, jolting me out of my thoughts. I halted in mid-step when Bramble the elf peered at me from the bushes. "You're in trouble, aren't you, Blair Wilkes?"

"Not as much as Oak is," I said. "Did you know he was living here in Fairy Falls without telling the witches?"

"Is that the fairy who's been hanging around our part of the forest?" he said. "Yes, I know of him."

I groaned. "You're really not helping me try to convince the witches that you aren't all tricksters, you know."

"Tricksters we might be, yet liars we are not."

"What does that even mean?" I suspected that Mrs Hansen's beliefs went deep enough that it was unlikely I'd be able to convince her otherwise, while the stories I'd read in those books from the library had done little to instil confidence in me that the fairies would ever be human enough for her—or for the others who shared her opinion.

The elf ducked back into the bushes without answering me, leaving me more confused than ever.

13

I couldn't avoid going home forever. Eventually, I trailed back to the main part of the town with a cloud of shame hanging over my head. To make matters worse, it started to rain on the way back, too, so I arrived at my door dripping wet. I applied a quick drying spell to get rid of the water before I entered the flat, where I found Alissa and Nina in the living room with the cats. Sky approached me as soon as I walked in to steal a stroke from me.

"How'd it go?" Alissa raised her brows at the sight of me, from which I concluded that drying myself off hadn't hidden the mess the rain had made of my hair.

"I screwed up," I admitted. "Majorly."

"I heard what happened at the meeting," Nina said in sympathetic tones. "That Mrs Hansen interrupted to tell everyone to kick the fairies out of town, right?"

"Please tell me Madame Grey told her to get stuffed," added Alissa.

"Not exactly," I said. "Somehow, Mrs Hansen found

out that there's a fairy living in town who hasn't announced himself to the witches yet and decided to announce it at the meeting. He's been here a while, but he doesn't trust the witches or anyone else either."

Alissa groaned. "Oh, Blair. Tell me you didn't know he was there."

"Okay… I won't tell you." I slumped into an armchair, where Sky promptly climbed onto me. "When I tried to convince him to introduce himself to Madame Grey, he threw me in a pit and dropped an illusion of a net on me. Buck too. I really tried, but I didn't know Mrs Hansen knew he existed until she conveniently brought him up at the meeting."

"So you think she knew beforehand?" Nina guessed.

"I know she did, but I thought…" I stroked Sky, struggling to find the words. "I thought she was using him for her anti-fairy protest and that they were working together."

"You thought she worked *with one of* the fairies?" said Alissa.

"It made more sense in my head," I said, flushing. "Oak was the exact definition of everything she was complaining about. He refused to introduce himself to anyone, and he hid out of sight, playing tricks on people with his magic. Then she turned out to have been aware of him all along, so I had to wonder if they knew one another. It's not like he seems all that attached to the town. He said he's only here to stick it to the witches who sent the fairies away all those years ago. It didn't seem that implausible that she hired him in order to use him as an excuse to scapegoat all the other fairies."

"Okay, that's fair," said Nina. "I take it she wasn't happy at you accusing her of kidnapping her own kid?"

"I didn't say that directly, but she's even less thrilled with me than she already was," I said. "Oh, and she's wearing some kind of charm that makes her immune to vampire mind reading, so she's not exactly acting as though she doesn't have something to hide."

Alissa's mouth parted. "Really?"

"Where'd she get hold of that?" asked Nina. "I didn't even know such a thing existed."

"Nor me," I said.

"Um." A flush spread across Alissa's cheeks. "Samuel mentioned there's a new charm that's all the rage in some other magical towns among people who work in close proximity with vampires. Maybe that's what she used."

"Samuel knew?" I didn't think he'd met Mrs Hansen face-to-face, but if he knew those charms existed, then Vincent must as well, which made the way he'd dismissed my concerns even more grating.

"He didn't know Mrs Hansen was using one," said Alissa. "I don't think he's ever met her. I doubt anyone expected her to crash the council meeting either. The others didn't cave in to her demands, did they?"

"No, but Madame Grey is confronting Oak as we speak," I said. "I hope he doesn't attack her."

"He ought to have more sense," said Alissa. "If not… well, then maybe he's better off leaving town after all."

"Except that's exactly what Mrs Hansen wants," I said. "As soon as he leaves, she'll think she's won, and she'll start pressuring the witches to drive off the others too. And I still don't know where her kid disappeared to. I was sure she was using Laurel to further her attempts to drive off the fairies."

"You thought she arranged her kidnapping?" said Nina. "By asking one of the fairies to take her?"

"Or her ex-husband," I added. "He seemed to be more sensible than she is, though it might've been for show. She's far more concerned with getting the fairies out of town than getting her daughter back. I don't know. It's all suspicious to me."

Not that I'd be making any more accusations until I had something resembling proof.

"Nah, I doubt she did," said Alissa. "She just knew how to take advantage of an opportunity."

"But we don't know where Laurel vanished to... or Rhiannon now too," I said. "*Her* parents didn't show up to the meeting, at least, but Rodney and the others have more cause to feel their concerns are legitimate."

"What exactly do they think the fairies are doing?" asked Nina. "Kidnapping children? Is that why you have that library book?"

I glanced at the book, which I'd forgotten I'd left out on the table. "Yeah, I figured I'd see where all these stories started. I also wondered if Mrs Hansen's hatred of fairies began before her child disappeared given how quickly she jumped to the conclusion that they were responsible. That's why I thought..."

"You thought she and Oak had an arrangement?" said Alissa. "I guess that sounds like something a manipulator like Mrs Dailey would do, but I'm not sure Mrs Hansen would do the same."

"Mrs Hansen is acting in a way that reminds me of her given her stunt at the council meeting," I said. "She even suggested the hunters were right, even though their leader was a fairy in disguise himself. She's so wrapped up in her hate that logic escapes her."

"I think it sounds like finding the missing children is the only solution, then," Alissa said. "Whatever truth it reveals."

My chest tightened. "You mean, whether it turns out the fairies did it or not."

It couldn't be, though. Oak clearly hadn't, and I'd questioned the other fairies myself.

At that moment, my phone buzzed with a message from Nathan, in which it sounded as if he'd gone to look for me after the council meeting. He must have just missed me, because my dad and I had taken off immediately afterwards. I texted him back, telling him I was at home, then looked up at Alissa. "It's Nathan. Glad he's not at the police station, because Steve's probably having to deal with Mrs Hansen yelling at him about my accusations."

"Serves him right," said Alissa. "He's the one who's supposed to be searching for the missing children. It doesn't sound like the police have done nearly enough."

"True," said Nina. "From what my mum said, it doesn't sound like they're about to take any drastic action against the fairies either. It'd take much more than one person's unfounded accusation to achieve that."

I nodded, still not feeling much better, and returned the library book to my bedroom before Nathan knocked on the door. As I went to let him in, I cringed inwardly at the thought of having to explain what a monumental mess I'd made of things all over again, but when he pulled me into a hug, I instantly felt better. "Hey, Blair."

"I screwed up," I blurted. "I suppose you heard all about it."

"I wouldn't mind hearing your side of the story," Nathan said.

"Mrs Hansen showed up and announced Oak was hiding in the forest to everyone at the council meeting," I said. "Because of the timing, I thought Mrs Hansen and Oak were working together and that she convinced him to 'kidnap' Laurel in order to have the fairies driven out of town and depose the covens at the same time. Turns out I got it completely wrong. Mrs Hansen forced Madame Grey to go to ask Oak to register his presence with the witch covens and then tried to ambush him beforehand. I managed to make the situation worse when I tried to drive her off, so I can't imagine their meeting went well."

"Actually, it sounds like it went as well as it could have gone," said Nathan. "From what I heard, anyway."

"Wait, she told you that?" I said, disarmed.

"No, Steve did," he said. "He met Madame Grey when she was on her way back from the forest. He seemed quite interested in the events of the council meeting, too, unfortunately."

"That figures," I muttered. "I suppose he wants to see how he can use the situation to his advantage. It's not like he particularly wanted the fairies to come and live here, either, considering how much he dislikes me."

"Steve hasn't even got the support from most of the gargoyles at this stage," he said. "He has Laurel's disappearance hanging over his head, but a fair few of the gargoyles have irrational superstitions about the forest and refuse to go further than the threshold. That's made it hard for them to search in depth."

"Please tell me Mrs Hansen's superstitions haven't been rubbing off on them." I caught sight of Erin and Buck approaching the house and waved them over. "Hey, Erin. Hey, Buck."

"Hey, Blair." Erin caught up to her brother, her hands buried in the pockets of her thick coat.

"Did you follow me here?" asked Nathan.

"You bet," Erin said. "We're not on duty. Plus I figured Blair would want to know that fairy left town."

"Which… which fairy left?" My throat went dry. "Not Oak?"

"If he's the one who threw Buck into a trap, then yes," she said. "I can't say I'm sorry."

"He left town?" I echoed. "For real?"

"Apparently, he claimed he knows he's not welcome here, so he decided to leave," said Buck. "I won't lie; it'll make our lives easier. I can't say I want to fall into a fairy trap every time I have to go into that part of the forest."

"But… that's exactly what Mrs Hansen wanted." *Oh, no.* "If he left, what's to stop her from trying the same with the others?"

"The others have introduced themselves to Madame Grey," said Erin. "All of them have shown they actually want to live here and get to know the other residents of town."

"That hasn't stopped her from accusing them of kidnapping her child," I pointed out. "I'm not saying she'll succeed in driving them out, but she's been doing her best to make them feel unwelcome and so have her allies. Would you want to live somewhere people protest against your existence outside your house every day?"

Erin's expression turned unusually sober. "I heard Mrs

Hansen kicked up a fuss at the council meeting, and that's what prompted this. Is it true?"

"You've got it," I said. "She knew Oak was in the forest and decided to tell Madame Grey in front of an audience to prop up her claims that the fairies are all tricksters. I went to warn Oak of Madame Grey's impending visit, but he didn't take it well. We can't let him leave town."

Nathan's brows shot up. "You want to bring him back?"

"I want to try." I backed into the house again, ready to grab my coat. "He's lived in this town longer than I've been alive, and he deserves to be here as much as anyone else."

"Wait, how old is he?" Erin asked as I shrugged my coat on and then grabbed my bag.

"Very old," said Buck. "I can't say I'm keen to make an enemy of him, Blair. Sorry. That illusion of his was nasty work."

"He thought he was being attacked," I explained to Erin. "He doesn't trust the covens. You don't have to come with me, any of you."

I knew this was a bad idea, but I'd been the one who'd truly been responsible for him leaving. Not Mrs Hansen and not Madame Grey.

In the end, Nathan refused point-blank to let me go alone, while Buck and Erin wouldn't stand in our way. It wasn't until Nathan and I reached the forest that the obvious hit me: I hadn't the faintest idea which direction Oak had gone in.

"I'll ask the other fairies," I said to Nathan. "Maybe my dad's around too."

I found the right path more easily than I had before,

walking towards the fairies' idyllic clearing. Before I could get any closer to their houses, however, I found my path barred by none other than Conor.

"You dare to show your face here, Blair, after you failed to defend us in front of the witch council when they decided to debate whether or not to drive us out of town?"

"I didn't—it was only Oak whose name came up in front of the council, and nobody wanted him to leave." My heart slammed against my rib cage. "I came here to convince him to come back to town. Madame Grey never intended to drive him away."

"I heard different," he said. "I heard the witches forced him to leave, at Mrs Hansen's request."

"That's not true," I told him. "I should have been the one to tell the covens he was here, but I kept quiet in the hopes that I might be able to convince him to go and introduce himself to Madame Grey in person. Instead, he used his magic against me and against a friend of mine. When Mrs Hansen inevitably found out he was there, she decided to expose him in front of the council. None of us had any idea she knew."

Conor's eyes narrowed. "I heard you undid his glamour, Blair."

"It was an accident," I squeaked, alarmed at the lightning crackling at his fingertips. He wouldn't turn *me* into a tree as a punishment, would he? "He and Mrs Hansen were about to start a public duel. I tried to warn him the covens would want him to tell them of his presence here in town, but he refused to listen until it was too late."

I should have known the other fairies would get mad at me, but I hadn't expected it to hurt so badly. When

Conor didn't speak, I said, "I'm sorry. I screwed up. What can I do to convince Oak to come back?"

"You can try to catch him," he said, "but you'll fail."

"That's not helping," I said. "Can't you contact him? You knew he was here from the start, right?"

"Yes, I did," he said, "but I am not the person who needs to convince him that he has a place here. That job goes to those who drove him away."

Ouch. "Can you at least give me a clue about where he went?"

He stepped back. "Start at his home."

As he vanished among the clearing, I turned back to Nathan. "I think that means we're too late."

"It's worth looking."

"If I can even find his house. It's hard to pin down." All I knew was that his house lay east of here, towards the lake, so I set off in that direction. Failure lay like a crushing weight on top of me as I walked, hand in hand with Nathan, until we came to the spot near the lake where I thought the path ought to lie.

Nothing remained except for an abandoned shack nestled between the trees. Oak was nowhere to be found. We'd arrived too late. He'd long since disappeared, as if he'd never been there at all.

14

It was impossible for me to think of Oak's departure as anything other than proof of my own failures. While he'd always been unwilling to cooperate, it was my actions that had ultimately caused him to leave town. Even if I managed to figure out which direction he'd gone, he clearly didn't want to be followed, least of all by me.

In the end, I returned home, while Nathan went to check in with Steve. Nina had gone back upstairs to her own flat, while Alissa had a shift at the hospital, which left me alone to mope—or rather, reread the book I'd checked out from the library, since it was that or spend the rest of the day dwelling on my own failures.

A loud hiss from Sky made me look up from the page. The cat's eyes were fixed on the pixie, who'd entered the room silently and scattered glitter all over the floor on the way.

"Oh, hey," I said to the pixie. "Didn't see you there."

"*Miaow*," Sky grumbled, which probably meant 'go away.'

The pixie ignored him, fluttering down to my side in a sweep of wings that caught the library book and sent it toppling off the edge of the sofa, where it landed face down on the floor.

I leaned over to pick it up and saw that a scrap of paper had fallen out of the book. I retrieved the paper, on which someone had scribbled the words, *Use this one.*

With my other hand, I picked up the book and flipped it open to the page someone had marked with the scrap of paper. The heading read *Changelings and began the part of the book detailing the various myths of fairies capturing human children.* Changelings, according to the text, were fairy children left in the place of a human child, each of which looked identical to the child they replaced. As the stories claimed, the child's parents often knew something was wrong, but they were rarely able to prove that the child wasn't theirs, not when the people around them didn't believe fairies even existed.

I looked between the note and the page, wondering who'd wanted to mark out this particular section, and Mrs Hansen's face came to mind. For all her insistence that fairies had captured her child, she'd never mentioned the second part of the story... namely, the notion of a fairy child being left in place of the missing human one. Had she decided that part of the story didn't apply to Laurel Hansen's disappearance? Or... wait, when we'd first met, she'd accused the fairies of kidnapping children and leaving their own substitutes, changeling-style. Yet she'd never clarified what she meant by that.

I rose to my feet, struck by the sudden desire to go to

the campus and ask Samuel if he knew who might have been the last person to take out this book. The campus would be deserted at this time, but if anyone would be lurking in the library when nobody else was around, it was the library vampire.

Sky growled his disapproval at being left behind, but I threw him some treats before leaving the flat with the book tucked under my arm. The pixie accompanied me part of the way through town, flitting at my side for a while before disappearing from sight again when I entered the campus itself.

At the weekend, the campus seemed oddly deserted. While loud music drifted from the direction of the student halls, hardly anyone seemed to be around, and I reached the library without encountering another soul.

Samuel didn't look surprised in the slightest to see me walk in. "Is there something you need, Blair?"

I held out the note. "This was inside the book I took out the other day. Do you know who wrote it?"

He read the words on the scrap of paper. "I can't say I do."

"Who was the last person to take out this book, then?" I asked.

"That I can look up." He moved behind the desk with a vampire's elegant grace, flipping open the record book. "Hmm. That book hasn't been checked out in a few months."

"Then… did a student pick up the book to study here in the library and then leave the note behind?" I'd been sure Mrs Hansen's name would crop up, but where had her fairy obsession started if not here? "I thought Mrs Hansen might have been the one who took it out."

"What would give you that idea?" he asked.

"Mrs Hansen is obsessed with fairies," I said. "Specifically, fairies kidnapping human children, which is the subject of the page someone bookmarked in that textbook I found. I always thought it seemed weird that she'd fixate on the idea of child-kidnapping fairies and then her actual child would disappear not long after."

"You mean suspicious," he said. "I understand why you would suspect foul play given the circumstances... and given her recent outburst at the council meeting."

"Are you reading my thoughts?" Wait. "At the meeting, Mrs Hansen wore some kind of charm that stopped her mind from being read by vampires. Is there a reason she might have chosen to do that? I thought it was fairies she was afraid of."

"I've never met her," he said. "Nor have I seen her on campus or in the library either. I imagine I would have noticed."

Then a student must have left the note. Rodney or one of his friends, perhaps, given that I'd seen them in the folklore section myself. "Have you seen Rodney and his friends lately, then?"

That brought a fanged smile to his mouth. "Yes. They tried to organise another meeting in the library, but I kicked them out for making a mess of the carpets."

"Serves them right," I said. "Ah... did you read *their* thoughts?"

"Like I said, I prefer not to invade my students' privacy," he said. "From what I saw, however, none of them knew anything of the missing children."

"Really?" Another theory bit the dust. "You *could* read their thoughts, though?"

"I could, yes."

Then they hadn't used the same charm Mrs Hansen had, which meant she'd got it elsewhere. From what I'd seen, they were obsessed with fairies alone and not vampires, but there seemed no obvious reason for her to protect herself against both.

"Okay," I said. "See you later."

I walked out of the library, my thoughts running in circles. Mrs Hansen thought her child had been taken by fairies, but she couldn't have been referring to one of the marked stories in the textbook. After all, there was no fairy child substitute, right? Someone would have noticed if there was. Besides, her house was covered in fairy-proof flowers.

Then there was the other family to think of too. Had they been dragged into this by sheer accident, or did they know more than they let on? If I wanted to find out, I'd have to visit them in person. Or I could ask Steve, but he was as likely to give me permission to conduct a questioning as he was to invite the fairies to a party. Whatever the case, it seemed as if all the pieces of evidence were drifting further and further apart like icebergs, and the truth was more distant than ever.

I found myself heading in the direction of the forest, my feet carrying me there of their own accord until I came to a halt near the street where Mrs Hansen—and the Bradley family—lived. After a brief scan of the area to make sure no gargoyles would come swooping in, I then headed down the road, keeping an eye on the purple-flower–covered house in case Mrs Hansen appeared and I needed to make a quick exit. Luckily, I reached the Bradley family's house without hearing her strident voice.

Maybe she was back at the police station again. The Bradley family might be, too, but it was worth seeing if they were in, so I knocked on the door before I lost my nerve.

Mrs Bradley answered, eyeing me in surprise. "Oh… you're that girl who was at the police station the other day. Can I help you?"

"I'm Blair Wilkes," I said. "I have a couple of questions I wanted to ask you. Um, about your daughter."

Her husband stepped up behind her. "Why do you want to speak to us?"

I drew in a breath. "Did your daughter know Laurel Hansen?"

"Why do you ask?" He frowned.

"They both disappeared in the same part of the forest, and you live on the same street, so I wondered," I said. "Did you ever speak to Mrs Hansen?"

"No, but… well, her daughter was friendly with Rhiannon," said Mrs Bradley. "They used to play together a few times before Mrs Hansen started acting weirdly about fairies."

"Was she always like that, then?" I asked. "Obsessed with the fairies, I mean?"

"I can't say I know," said Mrs Bradley. "We didn't speak to each other much before she split up with her husband, but it was nice for Rhiannon to have a friend her own age. We adopted her from foster care, you see, so she was new to town and pretty shy with the other kids."

"Ah, okay," I said. "Also—um, have you ever had contact with Pierce Reynold? Mrs Hansen's ex-husband?"

"Not since he lived here, and that was—what, five years ago?" Mrs Bradley glanced at her husband for confirmation. "Her daughter was very young when he left, anyway."

Hmm. Pierce Reynold was still tentatively on my suspect list, but I hadn't a clue where *he* lived, and I was pretty sure the Bradleys wouldn't either. Besides, nobody except for me had the ability to sense a person's paranormal type, so they wouldn't have any reason to be suspicious that he was hiding something. When put together with Mrs Hansen's charm to block vampire mind reading, something was plain odd about the pair of them.

"Yes, she was," said Mr Bradley. "Why are you asking us all these questions, anyway? Are you with the police?"

"No, I'm not," I said. "I've been helping them look for your daughter, though. Um, thanks for answering my questions."

They retreated into their house and closed the door behind them, leaving me slightly deflated on the doorstep. I hadn't even had time to ask them if they knew Rodney and his friends, but while I'd confirmed that Laurel and Rhiannon had been friendly with one another, that didn't prove anything.

As I turned to leave, my gaze caught on Mrs Hansen's house. As tempting as it might be to take a closer look, I'd probably end up accidentally walking into the fairy-proof flowers, so I left the street and made my way back towards the high street.

By a rare streak of luck, Nathan was leaving the police station as I walked past.

"Blair?" he said. "I thought you went home."

"I did," I said. "Then, ah, I went to speak to Samuel at

the campus library. Someone left a weird note in that library book I checked out."

"Weird how?"

"I don't know." I rubbed my forehead. "Has Steve got any more theories? Are the gargoyles even searching the forest anymore?"

"Supposedly, it's their day off." A scowl appeared on his mouth. "Why? Did you want to have another look around the forest?"

"Why were you there, then?" I asked. "Did Steve have nothing to say about the case at all?"

"Nothing except that he wishes Mrs Hansen's ex-husband was still in town, because at least when he was around, she had someone else to direct her ire at."

"Speaking of whom…" I paused. "Is it weird that I still think he might be involved? He didn't set off my paranormal-sensing power when I looked at him. It drew a total blank."

"Wait, he didn't?" he said. "You never mentioned that before."

"I thought he was human at the time," I said. "Maybe he is, but the last time my powers failed to identify someone…"

"Was when you saw the Inquisitor," he finished. "That's not necessarily grounds to add him back to the suspect list—not according to Steve, anyway—but I wonder why he left town when he did."

"Do you have his number?" A wild theory entered my mind, even more so than the notion of Mrs Hansen and Oak working hand in hand—but Oak was gone, my chance to plead the fairies' case to the witches on the council had passed, and the only remaining way to secure the other fairies' future in this town was to solve the mystery of the missing children.

"No." His gaze travelled towards the police station. "But I'll see what I can do. Wait for me here."

Then he was striding away, while I hovered out of sight to wait for him and hoped Steve didn't raise a fuss. Luckily, Nathan reappeared within five minutes and handed me a piece of paper with a number scrawled on it. "I wouldn't tell Steve about this."

"Steve should have done a better job of handling Mrs Hansen." I took the paper he offered and retrieved my phone from my pocket. "Thanks, Nathan."

"Good luck, Blair," he said. "Let me know how it goes, okay?"

"Sure." It might be another dead end, of course, but with Pierce out of town, calling him was my only shot at finding out the extent of his involvement.

I walked out of hearing distance of the police station before making the call. Pierce picked up after a couple of rings. "Hello? Pierce Reynold speaking."

"This is Blair Wilkes, from Fairy Falls."

"Blair?" Surprise coloured his tone. "I didn't expect to hear from you."

"You're a vampire, aren't you?"

A moment passed. "Excuse me?"

"Mrs Hansen carries a charm to block mind reading. I couldn't think of any other good reason she'd do that, considering fairies can't read minds."

"Oh," he said. "It's no big secret. The other vampires know."

You hid your paranormal type from me, though. "You weren't born a vampire?"

"Few are," he responded. "Why?"

"I can tell what type of paranormal someone is by looking at them," I explained. "You registered as plain human to me."

"Ah." He sounded slightly embarrassed. "I have a charm for blocking glamour. I suppose it must block your magic too."

"Seriously?" That wasn't a pleasant revelation at all. I hadn't even known such a thing existed. "Why do you have one? Did you think you'd need to defend yourself against glamour?"

"At first?" he said. "Yes, I did. When I received Abigail's message claiming that our daughter had been replaced by a changeling, I came to town at the first opportunity. It wasn't until I got here that I realised the fairies were no threat at all."

"You… you *don't* think they're a threat?"

"I do not, but that's not the only reason you called me, is it?" he said.

"No," I said. "You knew Mrs Hansen's paranoia about fairies was getting out of hand, didn't you? You must have done. Why would she assume her daughter was replaced by a changeling?"

"We adopted Laurel when she was a toddler," said Pierce. "Vampires are sterile, so we always knew we'd have to adopt, and Abigail was happy with our decision. She adored Laurel. Spoiled her. Our split was amicable at first, but until this recent obsession that fairies took her child and replaced it with another one, I had no idea the thought had even crossed her mind."

My lie-sensing talent remained dormant. It seemed he spoke the truth.

"Then why did you leave town so abruptly?" I asked. "You don't know where Laurel is, do you?"

His pause went on a fraction too long. I gripped the phone hard, disbelief coursing through me. "You asked someone else to take her in… and you were happy to let the fairies take the blame for her disappearance?"

"I had to." His voice was low. "Abigail claimed someone had replaced our child with another. Her claims were so irrational that I did what I had to in order to keep Laurel safe. There was no way to remove the accusation against the fairies without giving away her location."

"What about Rhiannon, then?" Had he arranged for *her* 'disappearance,' too? "Her parents seem completely normal, yet she vanished in the same manner as Laurel did."

"Ah, I can explain."

"You'd better," I said heatedly. "Mrs Hansen is trying to drive the fairies out of town. She brought one of them to the attention of the witches' council, and he *did* end up leaving town because he no longer felt welcome here. Now it turns out the fairies are pawns in some power play between the two of you and you even decided to bring someone else's kid into it?"

"Not at all," he said. "The children were my primary concern. As for Abigail, I cannot say I know what's driving her, but it's hard to prove anything when she hides her thoughts from me."

"Those kids have been gone for days," I pointed out. "Did you plan for this to go on indefinitely?"

"No," he said. "Nobody else was supposed to be brought into the situation except for that other fairy. I don't know if you've met Oak…"

"You know him too?" I said, disbelieving. "Is *he* the one who hid the children? Because he just left town thanks to Mrs Hansen exposing him in front of the entire witch council."

"He did?" said Pierce. "He's the one I contacted to watch the children and send me updates, but I can't say I had any idea Abigail ever set eyes on him."

Oak was the one he'd entrusted to keep an eye on the children? Had his tantrum and attempt to leave town been a ruse? Nothing about Pierce's actions made sense to me, and yet my lie-sensing powers told me he spoke true. "You'd better come and explain everything in person. If you don't, then a lot of people who had nothing to do with the children's disappearances are going to take the blame."

If they hadn't already. Mrs Hansen was closer than ever to achieving her goal of getting rid of the fairies, but with Pierce who-knew-where, it looked as though I'd have to attempt to sort out this situation myself before it spun even further out of hand than it already had. If Pierce had given Oak the children, though, he *must* still be in the area.

I still had time to find him.

"I will endeavour to make it to town by tonight," he said.

"I'll hold you to that." Ending the call, I retraced my steps to the street bordering the forest, wondering if Oak was still somewhere among the trees after all.

I'd been right, in a way, when I'd suspected him of being involved… but he'd been working with Pierce and not with Mrs Hansen at all. Still, had neither of them cared if Mrs Hansen took out her anger on the other fairies? It sounded like Pierce had felt he'd had no choice but to remove the children from her sight, yet he'd also been as surprised as the rest of us at Mrs Hansen's sudden and irrational crusade against the fairies.

My gaze landed on her house and its flower-covered exterior, and I approached with a swift stride. Up close, a vivid glow shone underneath the windowsill and along the length of the house, bright enough that it would have been highly noticeable if not for the abundance of flowers. Weird.

I inched closer to the gate at the front and spotted a neat row of herbs scattered in front of the door in a line that continued around each side of the house. Had she set up another booby-trap in case a fairy tried to get into the house? I didn't recognise the herbs, so I snapped a picture and sent it to Alissa, asking her if she could identify them, before treading past the house and towards the forest.

I hadn't got far before Mrs Hansen herself stepped onto the path and halted in front of me. Her mouth pressed into a line, and her eyes darted over me in a manner that suggested her last thread of patience had come undone. "So you talked to my ex-husband."

15

How'd she guess? Maybe she'd overheard. Which meant she'd probably seen me snooping around her house, too, but that was the least of my worries.

"Yes, I did," I said to Mrs Hansen. "He told me some illuminating things about you and the child you mistreated because you believed she wasn't yours."

"I did nothing," she said. "Laurel is mine. The *real* Laurel is. The fairies have her, and I intend to get her back."

"Yeah, that's not how it works." *So it's true.* She honestly believed the fairies had taken her real child and left a substitute in her place. Pierce had better show up soon, because I wasn't entirely convinced that I could fend off Mrs Hansen on my own without doing more damage than I intended. Especially when I had zero clue where Oak was hiding and whether he'd jump to my defence.

Mrs Hansen raised her wand. "Not just my own child.

Mr and Mrs Bradley's child was replaced by a changeling too."

"Let me get this straight," I said. "You frightened Mr and Mrs Bradley into sending away their *own* child?"

Her face flushed with anger. "They took her. The fairies did. I only tried to enlighten them on the truth."

"I suppose they were too shocked to report you to the police," I said. "And it's not like there's a process for dealing with claims that someone's children were replaced by fairies, especially if they're complete lies."

"I'm not lying."

I didn't need my lie-sensing power to know that was total nonsense. "Did someone bewitch you? Why do you hate the fairies so much?"

Her obsession went far beyond an irrational belief fixated on the newcomers in town. Given my own bad experiences with the fairies at the goblin market, I couldn't deny some of them *were* capricious and cruel, the same way some humans could be. It was just unfortunate that in this particular case, her crusade against the fairies had had unintended consequences, especially for the two children who'd been caught up in this mess.

"You know why." A tremor underlaid her voice. "I don't have to listen to your accusations."

"Your ex-husband said you had no issue with fairies the last time you saw one another."

When my phone vibrated loudly in my pocket, I jumped, fumbling for it. Mrs Hansen remained frozen for an instant, as though she couldn't figure out where the sound was coming from, while I found a message from Alissa. She'd sent a response to the picture I'd taken of

Mrs Hansen's house: *That's an enchantment. Someone bewitched her house. I can't tell what they were trying to do.*

I looked at the phone then back at Mrs Hansen as comprehension dawned on me. No wonder she'd been acting so irrationally. Someone had put a spell on her. Someone like…

Rustling sounded amid the bushes, and Rodney and his friends walked into view, armed with their wands and with fairy-proof flowers around their necks. You would have thought carrying bright-purple flowers would make them look less intimidating, but that was definitely not the case. Especially when I hadn't a clue how to remove the enchantment they'd put on Mrs Hansen.

I should have known they'd had her under their spell the whole time.

"What are you doing here?" I demanded of Rodney and his friends. "Are you harassing the fairies again?"

"We're here to find the missing children," said Rodney.

"Is that why you're armed?" I didn't know how seriously he took the stories himself, but the guy had a definite screw loose. As for Mrs Hansen, I needed to get the spell off her before she and the others actually did find the missing children, wherever they were. Crossing my fingers behind my back that Pierce was moving here as fast as his vampire speed allowed, I stayed put, blocking Mrs Hansen's path.

"Get out of the way." She raised her wand, only for a sudden blast of lightning to skewer a nearby tree and knock the wand out of her hand.

I jumped back, alarm blaring through me, and spotted movement in the bushes. *Elves? Or fairies?* Whoever it was, their lightning bolt had sent Rodney and his friends scattering in a panic, so I went looking for my rescuers.

A pair of pointed ears popped up. "This way, Blair Wilkes."

From the bushes, Bramble the elf beckoned me to follow him. Out of any better ideas, I hastened after him down the winding path between the trees, bringing out my wings in the process to quicken my pace. Even so, the elf moved faster than me, and it wasn't until we neared the Elf King's domain that I caught my breath for long enough to speak.

"What is going on?" I said. "Do you know where the missing children are? Because Mrs Hansen and her new friends mean business."

Bramble came to a halt within sight of the Elf King's tree then veered around the side along a path I hadn't been down before. "We intended to keep the children safe from the likes of them."

"Then you knew." I should have guessed, really, from the way the Elf King had danced around the subject during our last encounter. "Mrs Hansen thinks her child was kidnapped by fairies, and the police have been searching the forest for days. You mean to tell me you knew where they were all along?"

How long had the elves been in on the plan? Pierce had given me the impression it'd been Oak who'd taken them, but I saw no signs of the crotchety fairy as we walked on down the winding path.

"It's complicated."

You're telling me. I followed him around another corner and came to a halt at a grassy clearing that shone around the edges with the gleam of fairy glamour. There, I saw two children chasing one another around the grass, supervised by two fairies. Conor was one of them. My dad was the other. When he spotted me, his expression went from surprised to sheepish.

I gaped at both of them. "You knew where the children were too?"

"No," said Dad. "Conor and I found out at the same moment… that is, when the elves saw fit to tell us."

"Bramble." I turned to frown at the elf. "You might have *told* me the children were safely here. I think the police would have been grateful to know too. Not to mention Rhiannon's parents."

"The children have no idea anything is going on," said Bramble. "They're not in distress. Mrs Hansen's behaviour made it necessary to remove the children from her sight."

"She's under some kind of enchantment," I said. "Rodney and the others put a spell on her. I didn't know until I saw the herbs outside her house and sent a picture to Alissa, who managed to identify them as part of an enchantment that somehow made her think her child was a changeling. What did you do, swipe Laurel from her back garden?"

"Mrs Hansen left her child in the woods, alone," said Bramble. "She wanted the fairies to take her back, so we complied."

"And Mr and Mrs Bradley's child?" I looked at the two children playing together in the clearing. "Why take her as well?"

"Because Rhiannon is a fairy changeling," he said. "Both of them are, in fact."

I stared at the two children, disbelief flooding me.

"Seriously? How is that even possible? The stories say the fairy changeling is a substitute for a human child, but… that's not what's happening here, is it?"

"The stories don't tell it all," growled the elf. "Some fairies have long made a practise of leaving their own children with humans in order for them to have a better life. No doubt that is how the legend originated. Both children you see were left with human families to be raised as their own."

My mouth fell open. "Does that mean they were raised without their parents knowing they weren't human?"

"Not at all," said Conor. "Their parents signed an agreement. It's a standard practice for those of us in the know."

It would have been nice if someone had enlightened me on that beforehand.

"Mrs Bradley said Rhiannon was adopted…" I broke off. "I guess she didn't want to break her agreement by telling me her birth parents were fairies, but what about Mrs Hansen? She *knew* she'd adopted a fairy child, yet she still ended up falling under Rodney's spell?"

"I would guess that Rodney and his ilk found out the children weren't human through their own sleuthing and then sought to use that knowledge to sow discord," said Bramble, disdain colouring his tone. "I cannot say what kind of enchantment they used on Mrs Hansen, but I would guess it made her forget she signed the agreement herself. Since we were unaware of the reason for her behaviour, we were forced to take in the children for their own safety."

"Without even telling the other fairies?" I looked to my

dad and Conor for confirmation. "You really didn't know?"

Oak did. Of course, the prickly fairy wouldn't share anything with the others, but I could hardly believe he'd trusted the elves instead.

"No," said my dad. "The changeling situation isn't one we've dealt with in a long while. Usually, it occurs in tragic situations like the one your mother and I found ourselves in, where we placed you in an ordinary human family."

"With good reason," I said. "Because you were in jail and you thought I'd be safer… *oh.*"

"Exactly," he said. "Laurel's birth family wasn't so different, and neither was Rhiannon's. Both families wanted their children to be given the best chance at a good life, and they went for years without anyone being any the wiser as to their origins."

"Until the fairies started coming back." Something else occurred to me. "If I'd looked at the kids up close, I'd have been able to tell they were glamoured, wouldn't I?"

"Yes," said Dad. "And so would I, but it wasn't the fairies they feared would discover them."

No. Rodney and his friends were the ones they needed to be afraid of.

"I guess not," I said. "I wouldn't have exposed them if they hadn't wanted me to."

"Of course not," said my dad. "I suspect your ability to see through glamour has strengthened as your magic has improved."

"Yeah… I wouldn't have been able to do any of this when I first arrived in the paranormal world," I allowed. "I'm glad I got the chance to learn about being a fairy without thinking I got kidnapped and placed among humans, at least." I hadn't read the changeling stories until later, of course, but they seemed more sad than sinister.

In the clearing, the two children continued to chase one another around, oblivious to the rest of us. They seemed happy enough, but I wished we could let Rhiannon's parents know she was safe without alerting Mrs Hansen or the others. We couldn't leave them in the forest indefinitely, either, but when Pierce returned to town, maybe I'd be able to find a way to get rid of the spell on Mrs Hansen and drive off Rodney and his friends.

As the thought crossed my mind, the sound of voices and footsteps crunching in the undergrowth drifted in our direction, too loud to belong to the elves. "I think they've found you."

"We cannot let them near the king." Bramble stepped forward, his hands crackling with lightning. "The punishment for attacking him is death."

"What?" Alarmed, I launched forward, half sprinting, half flying through the trees and towards the approaching noise. Mrs Hansen might have been driving me out of my mind all week, but she wasn't in her right mind herself and didn't deserve to be punished for what Rodney and the others had done to her. When the clearing vanished from sight, I caught up to their group, skidding to a halt in front of Mrs Hansen. "Stop. You're trespassing."

"Where is my daughter?" she demanded.

"You won't find what you're looking for here." It was true in a way. Besides, I didn't want Rodney and his friends near the elves' territory *or* the missing children.

Rodney himself came lumbering over. Before he could barge past me, I grabbed my wand and cast the first spell that came into my head. A jet of glittering water splattered him and his friends from head to toe, and as they recoiled, I snapped my fingers and used my fairy magic.

Glamour spread from my hand to the ground, turning it into a pit at their feet. They tumbled and flailed and tripped, and I silently thanked Oak for teaching me that trick. The pit looked so realistic that I had to remind myself I couldn't trip over the edge when I walked over to look down at Rodney and his allies. "Whichever one of you is putting a spell on Mrs Hansen, tell me how to take it off. Then I might consider letting you out of the trap."

"There's no trap." Rodney backed up a step before climbing out of the non-existent pit and advanced on me again. Before he could move far, however, he found himself surrounded by elves, all of whom carried pointed sticks. Unfortunately for Rodney, however, he'd managed to drop his wand at some point between getting soaked and falling into the illusory pit.

"Take the spell off her," growled Bramble, jabbing a finger at the bewildered Mrs Hansen. "Now."

"You can't lie to me any longer," I added. "I know what you're doing. You figured out there were fairy changelings in town and decided to get rid of them by bewitching their parents into giving them up to the fairies. You're despicable."

"I'm not bewitched!" Mrs Hansen claimed.

"I beg to differ."

I spun on my heel, seeing Pierce approaching our group at a fast pace. The vampire had good timing, that was for sure, though vampire speed was beyond what even a fairy was capable of.

"Who are you?" said Rodney.

"My name is Pierce." The vampire showed his fangs, and the group backed off a little. "Abigail Hansen's ex-husband. I have to say, you almost fooled me into thinking her behaviour was natural."

"You're a vampire?" Rodney paled. "I didn't know."

"Yes, I am." His fangs came out again, and the students all jumped violently when he covered the distance between them in the time it took to blink.

I cleared my throat. "Might want to tone it down a bit."

His ex-wife stared at him in disbelief, while Pierce continued to glower at Rodney. "If the spell you used on Abigail is what I think it is, then you'll be lucky to avoid spending a decade in jail, boy."

"You won't win this." Rodney's expression cleared as one of his fellow students passed him his wand. "Vampire or not, I can stop you, and I will. Mrs Hansen, that man isn't your husband. He's an impostor."

At once, Mrs Hansen straightened upright, the doubt and confusion vanishing from her features. "So I see."

How did he do that? The enchantment was on her house, right? But if he had the ability to influence her behaviour, he must have some means of doing so in his own hands as well. He'd left a bunch of herbs outside her front door... so where might he have hidden the other part of the spell?

The bright-purple flower pinned to his coat caught my eye, and before I'd quite thought through my actions, I cast the rain spell again. A jet of glittery water shot from the end of my wand and crashed into Rodney head-on, knocking the flower aside. For an instant, a transparent stream of light appeared, connecting Rodney and Mrs Hansen. Then Mrs Hansen let out a little gasp, and a sound like the faint noise of breaking glass resounded as

Pierce glided across the path and stamped, hard, on the flower, grinding it into dust.

Mrs Hansen's expression blanked as she stumbled back, lost for words. Then her gaze went to Pierce helplessly. "Laurel?"

"She's fine," he said.

Mrs Hansen sank down and began to sob. "I gave her away. What have I done?"

"It wasn't your fault." I glared at the group of students, who'd returned their attention to the vampire and the armed elves surrounding them, barring them from running away.

A moment later, a loud crashing noise sounded, like something very large and clumsy making its way through the bushes. Several gargoyles lumbered into view, led by Steve, who took in the scene before him with visible confusion. Who'd sent him here? Or had he finally decided to do his job?

"I'm told someone is causing trouble in the forest." His gaze went from me to the sobbing Mrs Hansen and to the circle of elves surrounding the students—and Pierce, who still had his fangs on full display. "Isn't this the elves' territory? What are you all doing in here?"

I indicated the students. "Rodney and his friends came here to start a fight with the elves."

"No, we didn't," he said. "You should be arresting her, not me. She threw glitter at me."

"In self-defence," I clarified, for Steve's benefit. "They also bewitched Mrs Hansen and convinced her to abandon her child, thinking it was a fairy changeling."

"Did they now?" He addressed Mrs Hansen, who kept on sobbing. I hoped she'd jump to my defence, but she seemed incapable of speaking a coherent word. Through sobs, she nodded, shuddering.

"Yes," said another voice. "It's true."

All eyes turned to the right as Oak walked onto the path to join our unlikely-looking gathering. I'd been wondering if he'd planned to show his face and explain his part in the elves' plan. His gaze, however, went straight to the fake trap I'd conjured up. "Who did that?"

Heat crept up my neck. "I did. Why?"

"It's not bad for a half human."

"Um." I hadn't the faintest idea what to say to that. "I thought you left town."

I'd thought this very group of people had driven him off, but it sounded as if *he'd* been the one who'd helped the fairies pick which human families would raise their children and then stepped in to help when Mrs Hansen had fallen under Rodney's spell. I was having a little difficulty connecting the dots between the prickly fairy who'd chased me off and someone who'd helped save the day, that was for sure.

"Not yet." He moved closer, revealing someone else on the path behind him… Madame Grey.

"You knew?" I looked between him and Madame Grey. "And you too?"

"Not until today," she said. "During our visit, Oak told me of his intention to leave town and then added further clarification on why he came back."

"To watch the children?" I frowned. "Why?"

"Because he's here to steal more of them!" said Rodney, but his words were no longer as heated as before, especially with the vampire, elves, and gargoyles staring him down. He knew he was beaten.

"I should know, because I was the one who helped place the changeling child in Mrs Hansen's care," Oak said. "Clearly, it was a mistake to stop watching the town for potential troublemakers."

So Mrs Hansen really *had* been watched by the fairies… but not for the reasons she'd thought. "Why did you not take her in yourself? Why leave the children with humans when you were in the area the whole time?"

Oak scowled at me. "I was under watch by the hunters. Something you can relate to yourself, I'm sure."

My heart dropped. "I'm sorry. And—for accusing you as well."

"It was necessary to maintain my deception," he said. "For the sake of the children. I do hope these humans have no intention of bothering them again."

Mrs Hansen's sobs grew louder, prompting me to look at her. "Will she be okay?"

"In time." Pierce strode over to her side to speak to her. I didn't hear the words they exchanged, because the gargoyles began to herd the students away under Madame Grey's supervision.

Things got slightly confusing then. The gargoyles had trouble trying to get around my illusory pit, so I snapped my fingers to remove the spell, which startled Steve so much that he tripped over his own feet and landed in a bush. While the elves snickered at him, Oak watched with amusement, and I had an inkling that only Madame Grey's stern glare stopped Steve from yelling at all of us.

After he'd detached himself from the bush and lumbered after the disgraced students and the remaining gargoyles, the leader of the witches approached me. "Blair,

I would like very much to see the children if you can take me to them."

With the police gone, the forest had returned to its former quietness, especially as Mrs Hansen had finally stopped sobbing and was exchanging more whispered words with her ex-husband, while the elves had mostly withdrawn into the surrounding forest. That left Oak, who watched from afar and who caught my eye and gave the faintest nod.

"Okay." I stepped forward. "This way. Um. I don't know if Mrs Hansen wants to see Laurel yet…"

"We will come," said Pierce.

The pair of them followed Madame Grey and me, while Oak brought up the rear of our odd group. Several elves appeared on the path as we walked, flanking us until we reached the clearing. At the entrance, Conor and my dad waited for us.

"Everything okay?" Dad said in concerned tones.

"It's all good," I told him. "The students have been arrested, and we undid the spell on Mrs Hansen."

"I knew you'd find a way." Pride filled his voice, bringing a flush to my cheeks.

Oak walked into view with Mrs Hansen and her ex-husband trailing behind him. It was then that the children noticed they had company.

Laurel bounded over to peer around Conor. "Hey… it's my mum."

Mrs Hansen froze on the path, her expression startled. "Laurel!"

Her daughter ran towards her with a cry of delight. "Is that Dad with you? You never said he was coming!"

Rhiannon approached more warily, shuffling over to

Oak as her friend ran to meet her parents. From the way she looked up at the older fairy with a trusting expression on her face, the two of them must have met before, but it made an odd contrast with Oak's former reclusiveness.

Beyond the reunited family, I spotted Nathan approaching along the path. With a brief nod to my dad, I hurried over to meet him. "There you are, Blair. I'm glad Steve got to you in time."

"You're the one who sent him here?" I said. "And he actually listened?"

"Wonders will never cease," he said. "Also, I hope you're going to explain why Mrs Hansen's here. I thought she was the one you were chasing."

"She was under a spell, thanks to Rodney and his friends," I explained. "Pierce helped to keep the children safe, along with Oak and the elves, until they could figure out what was going on with her."

"The elves," he said. "Of course. That's where the shoe was found."

"Might have been a deliberate clue they left for me," I allowed. "They wanted me to know the children were never captured at all."

Nor were they missing either. The children looked right at home among the fairies and the elves in a clearing made of glamour, and Mrs Hansen's expression held no fear as she embraced her daughter.

16

At work the following day, the office was bustling with activity. I'd finally finished my database and sent it to Veronica for approval, which left me at something of a loose end. There was plenty to do to help the others with their ongoing projects, though, and without the worry about the missing children lurking in the back of my mind, it was much easier to concentrate.

Veronica entered the room as I was taking a breather to pick up some coffee.

"Blair," she said. "Good job on the database. You've covered most of the key areas, I think."

"Thanks," I said. "I hoped it might make it easier for us to find suitable placements for more fairy clients in the future."

"Of course," said Veronica. "I have something of my own that I'd like to share with you. All of you, in fact. Check your emails."

There came the sound of clicking as all four of us

opened our inboxes and clicked on the latest mass email sent from Veronica's address. It contained a link to a database that listed all the fairy clients in the area... in particular, those who'd been adopted into human families.

My mouth dropped open. How had she even collated all this information? It must have taken days, though admittedly, she did share her daughter's ability to work at a speed beyond that of most normal people.

"I heard about the incident involving those 'missing' children," Veronica said. "I had a suspicion that it wasn't the first incident of the type, given that it seems to be common for fairies to leave their children with human families if they have no better alternative. Yet the children's experiences aren't always happy ones, and they don't always come out of it knowing how to navigate the human-run job market or how to find others of their kind."

I swivelled in my chair to face the boss. "You want me to help them find their way to Fairy Falls? Doesn't this go beyond our scope as a recruitment company?"

"That's what I was thinking," said Bethan. "Don't get me wrong, it's a great idea, but this is way out of our area of expertise."

"Giving them employment is our goal," Veronica said. "As for the rest, I thought the other fairies ought to be at the centre."

"You mean you want to give this information to them?" I had the suspicion Conor already had some of it, and so did my dad, but that didn't mean there weren't some fairies who hadn't heard of their brethren taking up residence here in Fairy Falls.

I looked back at the database again, which had also

categorised the fairies by skills varying across different disciplines. Highlighted was a column for those who had experience dealing with orphaned or abandoned fae children.

At that, I nearly burst into tears at my desk.

From what I'd heard, Mrs Hansen was brimming with remorse over what she'd done while under the influence of Rodney's spell, but Rhiannon and Laurel were only the beginning. While they had families of their own, there'd be others who hadn't ended up in happy circumstances, who'd need all the help they could get. They'd need help finding stable employment at the very least, which was one thing we'd be able to provide.

After the boss left the office, Rob spoke first. "I'm glad they found her. Laurel, I mean."

"I'm glad they found her a good home too." I swallowed around a lump in my throat. "I didn't know there were so many fairies in the foster system."

Maybe I should have, given my own experiences. But I'd got lucky with Mr and Mrs Wilkes, and I was more grateful than ever for that now. I made a mental note to call them tonight and then returned my attention to the others. "Will you be okay helping out with this?"

"Sure," said Bethan. "It's a good initiative."

"Exactly," added Lizzie. "I'll print out copies of the database to give to employers if you like."

"Good idea."

Considering the short notice, I was heartened by their efforts to help out. Then again, everyone had heard about the bewitchment placed on Mrs Hansen and the revelation that there'd been two fairy changelings living among us all along—but not for the reasons anyone would have expected. In fact, from the looks of things, there were more changelings in perfectly happy human families than I'd ever have guessed existed. Some, though, would want to know where they'd come from, and I'd be more than happy to help them.

There was a lot of work to be done.

———

When work finished for the day, it was time to go to my magic lesson. I couldn't say I was enthused at the prospect of another magical theory lesson after last week's, but I'd expected a change of subject from last time. Disappointment filled me when Rita turned back to the same page in the textbook as she had the previous week.

"Today, we're continuing with our lessons on the town's history," she said, her gaze landing on me. "With that said, I've been in touch with the regional coven, and they've agreed that we can make allowances for you, Blair, if you want to write about the fairies' involvement in the town's history during your exam."

My mouth parted in surprise. "Are you sure?"

"Of course," she said. "The textbook needs updating in the long term, but for now, the council has agreed that it's within the rules of the syllabus for you to focus your attention there."

I hadn't even thought about the exams I'd have to take when I eventually made it to the end of my Grade Four classes, but just knowing it would be a possibility to write about the fairies' role in the town's history raised my mood a notch.

"Thank you," I said, sincerely. "I'm glad, though I might

have to speak to Oak if I want to hear a first-person account of the events."

I was also glad that the other fairies who came to town would be allowed to do the same if they decided to enter the magical education system along with the other paranormals. Given our new efforts at Dritch & Co, it was good timing.

"We're also looking into introducing the updated history into the academy's lessons too," she added. "And at the university. I think that's a place where it's sorely needed."

"Yeah." Rodney's group had disbanded—not that they'd been very popular among their peers after the truth had come out about Rodney's association with the two missing children and with bewitching Mrs Hansen. On the other hand, the fact that he and his friends had been able to gather a following in the first place pointed at an issue that needed to be rectified.

Sending a silent thanks to Madame Grey for pulling through for me again, I returned my attention to Rita's lecture, and I got through the rest of the lesson in good spirits.

When I left the classroom, I found Samuel of all people waiting outside in the usual statue-like silence of a vampire.

"Whoa." I brought myself to a halt before I walked into him. "Did you want me to give the library books back?"

"Not at all," he said. "I simply wished to speak to you, Blair."

"About Rodney and his friends?" I guessed. "Did you know what they did to Mrs Hansen?"

"Not all of it," he replied.

"How much?" I said. "You said you didn't pick up on anything from their minds, but you threw them out of the library for a reason, didn't you? Did you know they were bewitching Mrs Hansen into abandoning her own child?"

"Mind reading is a tricky skill to utilise," he said. "Telling the difference between speculation and reality is difficult even for experienced vampires, since many people contemplate doing inadvisable things but don't follow through on them. Unfortunately, this case ended in the latter."

"You mean you can't punish people for *thinking* about doing bad things," I surmised. "Which is fair enough. I think those kids ought to have been disciplined for harassing the fairies, at the very least."

"That's out of my jurisdiction, unfortunately," said the vampire. "I can throw them out of the library but not the forest."

"Yeah, Steve needs to step up if he doesn't want the fairies to start taking matters into their own hands," I said. "Though at work, we're planning..."

"To help the local fairies adopted into human families find employment, I know," he said. "If any of them want to work in the library, I'm looking for an assistant, and I'd be delighted to help them."

"Oh," I said, surprised. "Thanks. I'll keep that in mind."

Out of the corner of my eye, I saw Nathan approaching. Samuel flashed me a fanged smile and stepped away. "Be seeing you, Blair."

"Hey." As the vampire vanished, I walked over to meet Nathan, greeting him with a hug and kiss. "Didn't know you were free."

"Steve let me take the evening off," he said.

"Generous of him," I commented. "So, we're going to the Troll's Tavern?"

"No… well, not yet," he said. "I wondered if the fairies might be ready to meet me."

I blinked at him. "You want to see them?"

"Yes," he said. "I want them to know that unlike Steve, I will work to defend them from people like Rodney and his friends. I also think we should recruit some of the fairies to our security team too."

"Oh, of course." I fell into step with him as we trod the well-known path to the forest's entrance. "Yeah, I was going to bring it up with Ani and Rosalyn, but it slipped my mind."

I almost didn't recognise Mrs Hansen's house when I walked past. The purple flowers had entirely gone, while the sound of laughing children echoed from the back garden. It sounded like Laurel Hansen and Rhiannon Bradley were playing together.

When I peered through the window, though, I saw Mrs Hansen… and Pierce. Huh. I'd thought he'd left town, but perhaps not. I turned away before she noticed me looking through the window and walked on.

As Nathan and I reached the forest, I spotted movement inside and saw none other than my dad roaming down the path. He came to a halt when he spotted us. "Blair?"

"Hey," I said, surprised to see him so close to the human part of town. "No problems?"

"I was just checking everything's okay with the children," he said.

"Looks that way to me," I said with a smile. "Nathan wants to meet the other fairies."

He arched a brow. "Including Oak?"

"Wait, Oak's back?" I hadn't had the chance to check up on the grumpy fairy since his surprise return to town. While he'd turned out to be more trustworthy than appearances had suggested, that didn't mean he'd necessarily be glad to see me. And how long would it be before he wanted to visit the children and freaked out Mrs Hansen all over again? I didn't know how fragile she was after her experience, though it looked as though Pierce was around to give her a helping hand for now.

"He is," said my dad. "I think he wants to be left alone. That's the impression I got."

"That's fine with me," I said.

As for the other fairies, Rosalyn and Ani still needed employment, though maybe they'd be interested in joining Nathan's security team. I'd ask them later. Afterwards, Nathan and I would have a double date that evening with Buck and Erin, who I was sure would want to help them out…

A buzzing noise from my pocket indicated a message… from my foster parents, telling me they were about to call me. Oops. I'd texted them as I'd left work saying I wanted them to call me later, not realising that I'd end up taking a detour into the forest after my magic lesson.

"One second," I told the others, tapping my phone screen. "Ah—hey. Sorry. I forgot I had to do something after work."

"Blair!" said Mrs Wilkes. "Is everything okay? Your last message had me worried."

"Sorry," I said. "Didn't mean to cause a panic. I just… had something unexpected happen."

"What is it?"

I hesitated then held a hand over the phone and turned to my dad. "I have a question."

"Oh?" he said.

I drew in a breath. "Would you like to meet my foster parents?"

ABOUT THE AUTHOR

Elle Adams lives in the middle of England, where she spends most of her time reading an ever-growing mountain of books, planning her next adventure, or writing. Elle's books are humorous mysteries with a paranormal twist, packed with magical mayhem.

She also writes urban and contemporary fantasy novels as Emma L. Adams.

Visit http://www.elleadamsauthor.com/ to find out more about Elle's books.